FATALE

ED BRUBAKER   SEAN PHILLIPS

FATALE

BOOK TWO
THE DEVIL'S BUSINESS

By ED BRUBAKER and SEAN PHILLIPS

Colors by Dave Stewart

MEDIA INQUIRIES SHOULD BE DIRECTED TO UTA - Agents Julien Thuan and Geoff Morley

IMAGE COMICS, INC.
Robert Kirkman - chief operating officer
Erik Larsen - chief financial officer
Todd McFarlane - president
Marc Silvestri - chief executive officer
Jim Valentino - vice-president

Eric Stephenson - publisher
Todd Martinez - sales & licensing coordinator
Jennifer de Guzman - pr & marketing director
Branwyn Bigglestone - accounts manager
Emily Miller - accounting assistant
Jamie Parreno - marketing assistant
Jenna Savage - administrative assistant
Sarah deLaine - events coordinator
Kevin Yuen - digital rights coordinator
Tyler Shainline - production manager
Drew Gill - art director
Jonathan Chan - design director
Monica Garcia - production artist
Vincent Kukua - production artist
Jana Cook - production artist
www.imagecomics.com

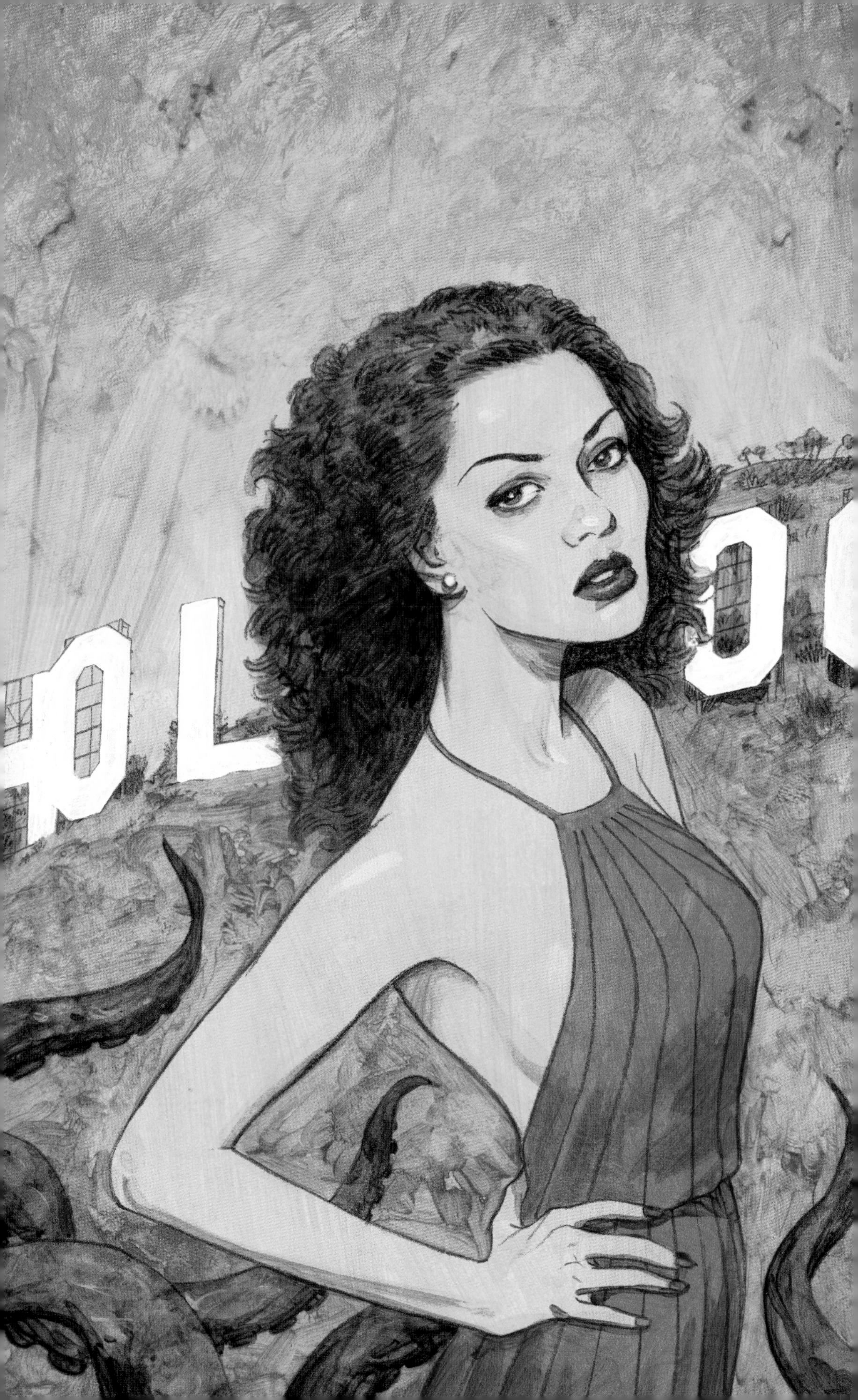

Prologue

Do crazy people *know* that they're losing their minds?

I'd wondered that a lot in the year since I'd lost my leg.

In the year since I'd become obsessed with *her*... with Josephine.

I say that because I *knew* I was obsessed... *And* I knew it was useless.

In all that time, I'd found out *nothing* about her. Not really.

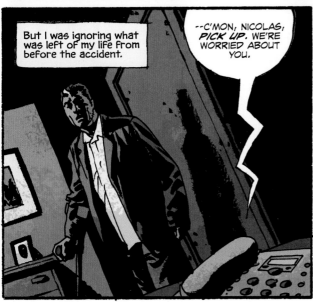

But I was ignoring what was left of my life from before the accident.

--C'MON, NICOLAS, *PICK UP.* WE'RE WORRIED ABOUT YOU.

And I'd practically forgotten my friends.

ME AND KEL JUST WANT TO KNOW YOU'RE OKAY...

All I thought about was *her*...

Or the *strange men* she'd saved me from that night.

Sometimes, I thought I saw one of them, out of the corner of my eye...

But I knew that was just part of my obsession.

The *paranoid* part.

THESE ONES GO UP TO *1972*, SIR... IS THAT *FAR ENOUGH*?

YES, THANKS...

I'd convinced uncle Dominic's publisher that I could write a biography of him...

So they were funding my research.

But I wasn't planning to write anything. I was just tracing the old man's life...

Desperately looking for any sign of Josephine in it.

Only once had I found anything even *close*.

Dominic had briefly lived in Los Angeles in the late '50s.

REPORTER TURNED MYSTERY WRITER HITS THE BIG TIME

Never before in History!

LIFE

And in a photo from a *Hollywood party*, there was someone who *might* have been her.

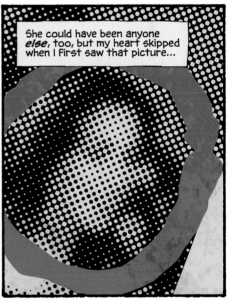

She could have been anyone *else*, too, but my heart skipped when I first saw that picture...

So I held onto that tiny hope.

And wasted months of my life staring at old industry and news magazines.

EXCUSE ME?

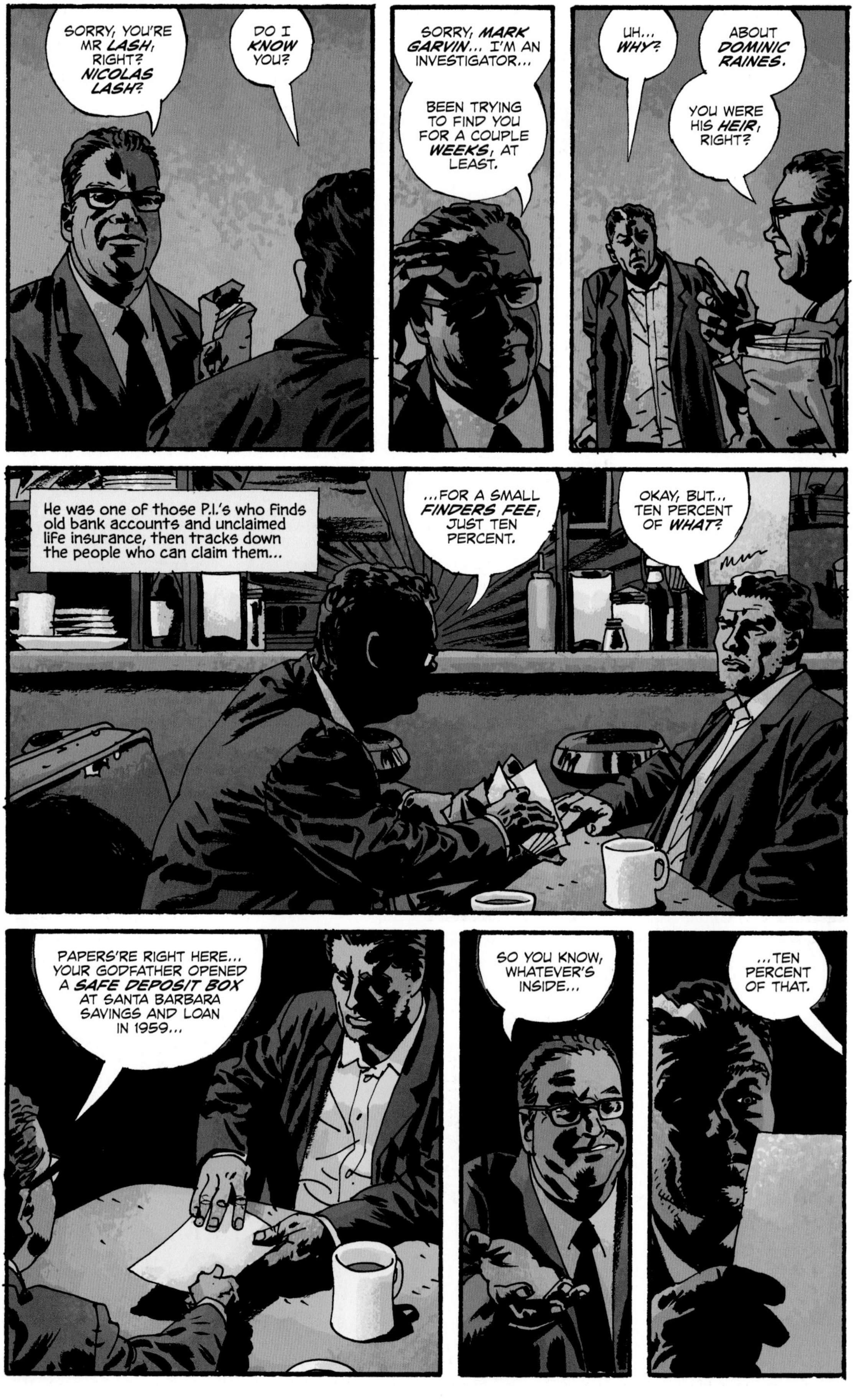
SORRY, YOU'RE MR LASH, RIGHT? NICOLAS LASH?
DO I KNOW YOU?
SORRY, MARK GARVIN... I'M AN INVESTIGATOR...
BEEN TRYING TO FIND YOU FOR A COUPLE WEEKS, AT LEAST.
UH... WHY?
ABOUT DOMINIC RAINES.
YOU WERE HIS HEIR, RIGHT?
He was one of those P.I.'s who finds old bank accounts and unclaimed life insurance, then tracks down the people who can claim them...
...FOR A SMALL FINDERS FEE, JUST TEN PERCENT.
OKAY, BUT... TEN PERCENT OF WHAT?
PAPERS'RE RIGHT HERE... YOUR GODFATHER OPENED A SAFE DEPOSIT BOX AT SANTA BARBARA SAVINGS AND LOAN IN 1959...
SO YOU KNOW, WHATEVER'S INSIDE...
...TEN PERCENT OF THAT.

Garvin says Dominic only visited the box once, but paid for it every year.

It was the lack of payment *this year* that put him on my trail.

So, after a year of no progress, something is finally going right.

MM HMM... OKAY MR LASH, ALL IN ORDER...

But of course, this is just another waste of time...

WHAT THE HELL... IT'S *EMPTY?*

WHAT?

WELL, MAYBE THAT *WOMAN* TOOK WHATEVER WAS INSIDE.

WHAT WOMAN? WHATTA YOU MEAN?

THE WOMAN *YOU* BROUGHT IN LAST WEEK, MR GARVIN.

TUESDAY, I THINK...

YOU *CAN'T* HAVE FORGOTTEN. I MEAN, YOU *WOULDN'T* FORGET *HER.*

And I don't even *need* the bank teller to describe this woman...

WHAT *IS* THIS, GARVIN?

DID *JO* PUT YOU UP TO THIS?

SERIOUSLY... NICK... I DON'T...

SANTA BARBARA
SAVINGS AND LOAN

I DON'T KNOW *WHAT* THAT GUY'S TALKIN' ABOUT...

I NEED TO CALL MY *PARTNER*, SEE IF HE... MAYBE...

JUST WAIT HERE, I'LL GET THE RENTAL CAR...

JUST...

The problem is, Garvin's *legitimately* disturbed.

And he'd have *no reason* to drag me down the coast for an *empty* box...

So what is –

HEY...

GET OVER HERE!

AHH!

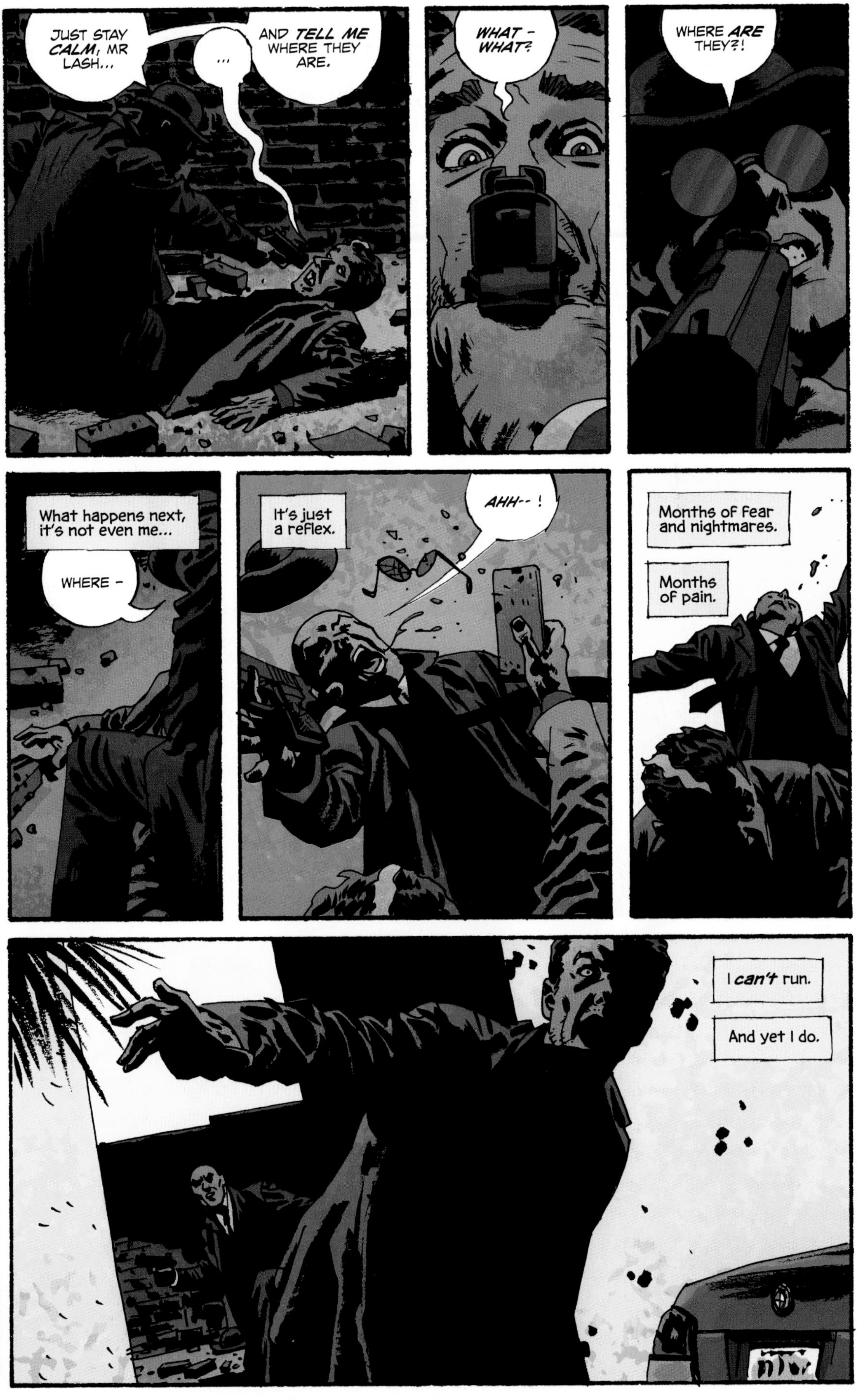

JUST STAY CALM, MR LASH...
...
AND TELL ME WHERE THEY ARE.
WHAT - WHAT?
WHERE ARE THEY?!
What happens next, it's not even me...
WHERE -
It's just a reflex.
AHH-- !
Months of fear and nightmares.
Months of pain.
I can't run.
And yet I do.

I run badly.

Like a cripple.

Like half of a three-legged race.

And that's what saves me.

AHH -- !

Or at least...

WHAT THE FUCK...?

...that's the *First* thing that saves me.

The *next* part happens so fast...

...I'm not even sure what I'm seeing.

GRAAAAHHHH -- !

Not until it's over.

And then it comes crashing down on me... the truth of it.

...HOLY FUCKING SHIT...

I wasn't being paranoid at all.

These fuckers *have* been following me.

All this time, all these months...

GARVIN...? YOU OKAY?

They've been right there in the shadows, waiting.

And I know now... I *know* that I'm *not* losing my mind...

SHIT.

But it sure as *hell* feels like I am.

Chapter One

Los Angeles –
Summer of 1978

SUPPOSEDLY, MILES HAD AN IN TO A PARTY AT NICHOLSON'S THAT NIGHT.

AS LONG AS HE WAS *HOLDING*.

THE *PROBLEM* WAS, HE WASN'T.

AND HIS REGULAR GUY WASN'T HOME.

SO HE HAD TO TRY A SOURCE HE'D RATHER HAVE AVOIDED.

FREE CONCERT NEXT SUNDAY. TAKE ONE... *HERE...*

THANKS.

HEY... YOU'RE A FRIEND OF *SUZY'S* RIGHT? *DARREN?*

DEREK.

RIGHT, WE MET AT THE THING, NEAR THE *OBSERVATORY...*

SURE. YOU'RE THE *QUITTER*.

NAH. I'M JUST NOT A *JOINER*, THAT'S ALL...

ANYWAY, THAT WAS FOREVER AGO.

SO, WHAT DO YOU WANT?

NEED SOME *BLOW*. SUZY USUALLY *HELPS ME* WITH THAT.

KNOW WHERE I CAN *FIND* HER?

THIS GUY WAS LIKE MOST OF THE *METHOD CHURCH'S* ACOLYTES, MILES THOUGHT.

JUST STUPID ENOUGH TO FEEL SUPERIOR.

YEAH, SHE'S AT SOME EVENT WITH BROTHER STANE...

I'M SUPPOSED TO MEET 'EM LATER.

BUT HE PUT UP WITH IT, BECAUSE HE HAD A PLAN.

CAN I GET AN ADDRESS? IT *IS* BUSINESS.

ASSUMING HE COULD GET TO THAT *PARTY*, AT LEAST.

THE ONE *GOOD* MOVIE HE'D EVER BEEN IN WAS PLAYING ON THE *LATE SHOW* TONIGHT.

AND HE HAD IT ALL WORKED OUT... HOW HE'D *ACCIDENTALLY* CHANGE THE CHANNEL...

HOW THEY'D NOTICE HIM ON THE SCREEN... THESE *IMPORTANT* PEOPLE.

THIS NIGHT WAS GOING TO BE HIS TICKET OUT OF SHITTY *B-MOVIES.*

ASSUMING HE COULD FIND *SUZY SCREAM,* WHO WAS AT A WHOLE DIFFERENT KIND OF PARTY.

CLEARLY, THE *METHOD CHURCH* HADN'T CHANGED, EVEN IF THEY *WERE* LESS VISIBLE THESE DAYS.

BUT HERE THEY WERE, AT SOME RICH *PERVERT'S* MANSION...

HEY, YOU SEEN SUZY?

PROBABLY SUPPLYING *HALF* THE GIRLS AND *ALL* THE DRUGS.

DOWNSTAIRS, I THINK...

THANKS. SORRY TO INTERRUPT.

THE LAST HOLDOUT FROM THE *DARK SIDE* OF THE *SIXTIES.*

AT LEAST THEY HAD GOOD *COKE,* HE THOUGHT.

UH... *SUZY?*

MILES?

OH *JESUS,* SUZE... WHAT THE FUCK *HAPPENED?*

I... I HAD... I *HAD* TO...

THEY WERE... *THAT.* THEY THOUGHT IT WAS *FUNNY...*

THEY FUCKING *DESERVED* THIS.

HOLY SHIT. THIS IS *BROTHER STANE.*

YEAH, HE *STABBED* ME... A LITTLE BIT...

JESUS... CAN YOU *WALK?*

WHAT DOES IT MATTER...?

THEY'RE GONNA KILL ME FOR THIS...

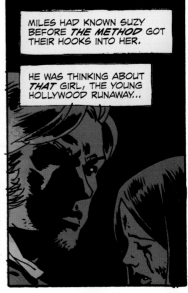

MILES HAD KNOWN SUZY BEFORE *THE METHOD* GOT THEIR HOOKS INTO HER.

HE WAS THINKING ABOUT *THAT* GIRL, THE YOUNG HOLLYWOOD RUNAWAY...

...WHEN HE FINALLY NOTICED WHAT THESE MEN HAD BEEN WATCHING.

...MY GOD...

OH, WOW... THEY'RE *HERE.*

WHAT?

HANS *ALREADY* KNOWS WHAT I DID... OF COURSE...

HE ALWAYS KNOWS...

WAIT RIGHT HERE.

CRAZY FUCKING GIRL, HE THOUGHT.

AND THEN HIS MIND EMPTIED...

AND REFILLED WITH COLD FEAR.

WHERE THE FUCK IS *BROTHER STANE*?!

WHERE *IS* HE?!!

C'MON, SUZY... WE GOTTA GO.

WE'LL NEVER — WE WON'T GET PAST THEM.

I *KNOW* THAT. BELIEVE ME.

SO WE'RE GOING ANOTHER WAY.

THE MANSION WAS PERCHED ABOVE A CANYON.

THE LAST UNTAMED WILDERNESS OF L.A.

HE PRAYED THE COYOTES WOULDN'T BE OUT TONIGHT.

Alan Marshal, like the others, never stood a chance.

He was a recovering alcoholic when I met him.

I flirted, but just once, so he'd help Hank sell his novel.

But two days after the deal closed, he was getting in drunken bar fights.

Soon he lost his clients, then his job at the agency.

He was forcibly removed from Hank's book release party, and that was the last time anyone saw him.

Until he washed up in the tide the next morning.

MS JOSEPHINE? MA'AM?

DID YOU WANT TEA? YOUR MOVIE'S ABOUT TO START.

OH, SURE, MONA... THAT SOUNDS NICE.

JOSEPHINE WAS, BY NOW, *OFFICIALLY* A RECLUSE.

SHE HADN'T EVEN BOUGHT HER OWN GROCERIES IN OVER FIVE YEARS.

NOT SINCE MISS JANSEN – MONA – HAD COME TO WORK FOR HER.

IT WAS JUST EASIER THIS WAY.

--TONIGHT'S FEATURE... *THE SQUEEZE PLAY...*

The Late Show

IF SHE STAYED AWAY FROM *MEN* AS MUCH AS POSSIBLE.

HERE YOU ARE, MA'AM.

THANKS.

THE ONLY THING SHE TRULY DESIRED ANYMORE THAT COULDN'T BE BROUGHT TO HER WAS THE OCEAN.

BUT ONCE IN A WHILE, SHE'D DRIVE OUT IN THE EVENING...

AND SWIM IN THE MOONLIGHT, WHEN NO ONE WAS AROUND.

EVERY NOW AND THEN, IT HITS HER THAT SHE'S BECOME THE WRONG HOLLYWOOD CLICHÉ.

WHEN THEY'D MOVED HERE, SHE THOUGHT ABOUT TRYING ACTING.

BUT IT TURNED OUT SHE HADN'T TRULY BEEN FREED IN SAN FRANCISCO. NOT OF HER *CURSE*, AT LEAST.

SO INSTEAD OF THE YOUNG *INGENUE*...

...SHE'D BECOME THE STRANGE *OLD LADY* WHO STAYS INDOORS AND WATCHES OLD MOVIES *EVERY NIGHT* ON TV.

EXCEPT SHE DOESN'T *LOOK* OLD.

SHE JUST *FEELS* IT.

AFTER HANK LEFT, THOUGH, THERE WAS A TIME WHEN SHE HAD BEEN FREE, IN A WAY.

SHE THOUGHT SHE'D LEARNED TO CONTROL HER EFFECT ON PEOPLE...

AND THERE WERE A FEW YEARS SHE ALMOST FELT LIKE A *NORMAL WOMAN* AGAIN.

BUT OF COURSE, IT HAD ENDED IN TEARS...

SHE HAD HURT TOO MANY PEOPLE...

AND BEEN HURT HERSELF MORE THAN SHE COULD BEAR.

AT LEAST *HANK* GOT OUT BEFORE THE WORST OF IT, SHE THINKS.

AND IT'S BETTER THIS WAY, SAFER... JUST HER AND HER MOVIES.

AND THEN TWO PEOPLE CAME CLIMBING OVER HER BACK WALL...

REMINDING HER THE *WORLD* MADE PLANS ALL ITS *OWN* SOMETIMES.

...OH...

SHE ALMOST CALLED THE POLICE... BUT SHE RECOGNIZED THE MAN.

SINCE HIS FACE WAS ON HER TV AT THAT *EXACT* MOMENT.

AND SHE'D BEEN ALIVE LONG ENOUGH TO KNOW *ONE THING* FOR SURE...

...IN *HER* LIFE, THERE WERE NO COINCIDENCES.

HEY... OVER *HERE*...

WAIT, LADY, WE'RE NOT --

PLEASE, COME IN... YOU'RE HURT, BLEEDING... YOU NEED HELP.

MILES... WHO IS THAT...?

PLEASE. IT'S OKAY... C'MON...

YOU CAN HIDE IN HERE.

MS JOSEPHINE? ARE YOU OKAY?

YES. I'M FINE... BUT THESE TWO AREN'T.

IT'S JUST SUZY WHO'S HURT... IT'S HER BLOOD...

WELL, FOR *GOD'S SAKE*, LET'S DON'T LET HER BLEED IN *HERE*...

COME ON, GIRL... WAKE UP...

HERE. I'LL TAKE YOUR COAT. YOU GO WITH MISS JANSEN...

BUT...

IT'S ALRIGHT.

SHE USED TO BE A *NURSE*.

SHE SEES IT IN HIS EYES...

...THAT HE DOESN'T UNDERSTAND WHY HE'S *LISTENING* TO HER.

AND SHE ALMOST FEELS BAD, BUT JUST ALMOST.

OKAY... WHAT'RE YOU CARRYING HERE...?

A *GUN?*

A *MOVIE?*

OF *COURSE,* SHE THINKS, THE MAN FROM THE MOVIES BRINGS A FILM.

AND WHEN SHE SEES THE SECRETS ITS FRAMES ARE KEEPING...

SHE *KNOWS* SHE WAS RIGHT.

IT *WASN'T* A COINCIDENCE HE WAS CROSSING HER PATH.

OH, I KNOW *EXACTLY* WHAT THIS IS, MISTER...

AND YOU'RE GOING TELL ME EXACTLY WHERE IT *CAME* FROM.

OH, HEY... YOU SHOULDN'T BE LOOKING AT THAT.

THAT'S NOT...

Chapter Two

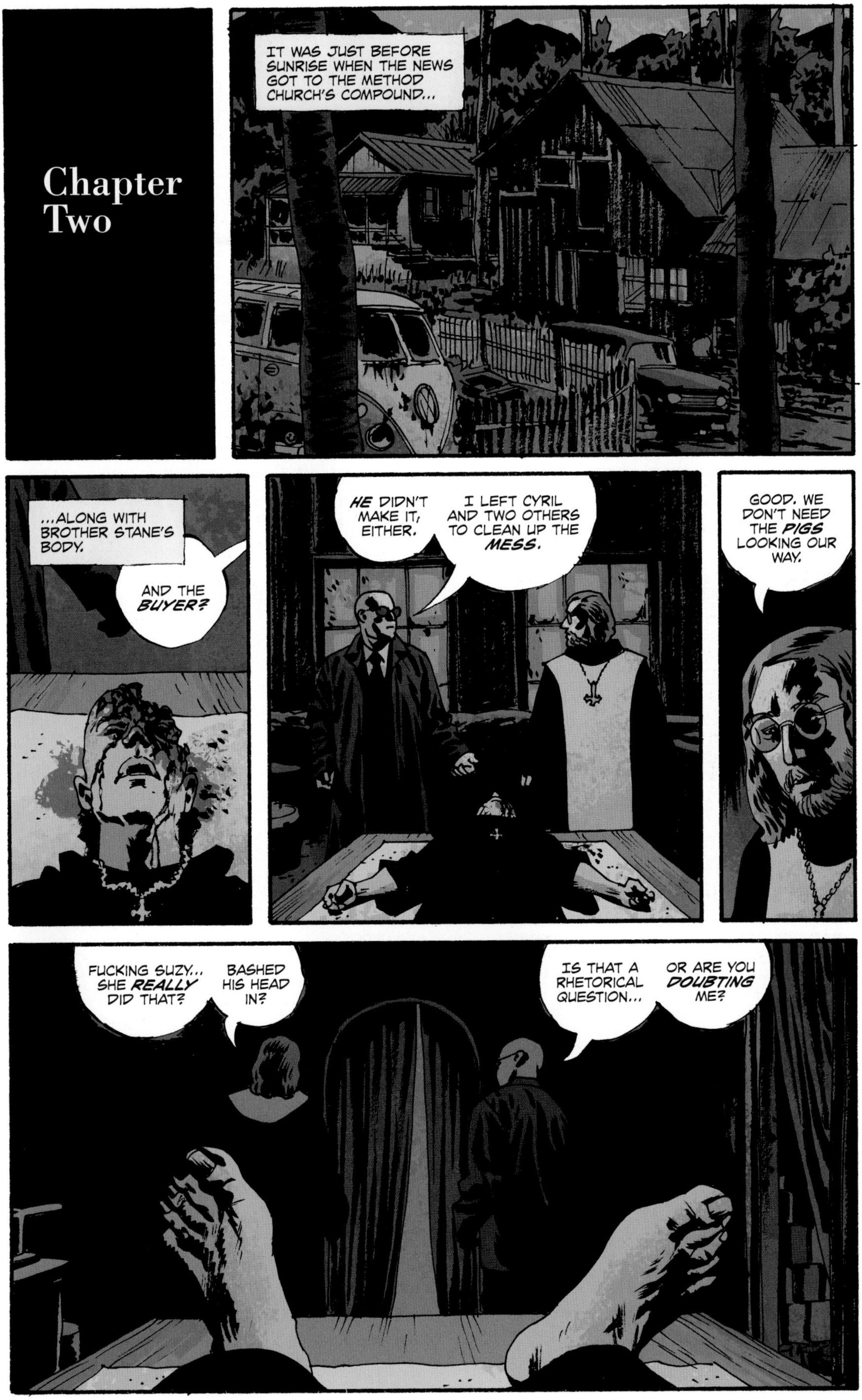

IT WAS JUST BEFORE SUNRISE WHEN THE NEWS GOT TO THE METHOD CHURCH'S COMPOUND...
...ALONG WITH BROTHER STANE'S BODY.
AND THE BUYER?
HE DIDN'T MAKE IT, EITHER.
I LEFT CYRIL AND TWO OTHERS TO CLEAN UP THE MESS.
GOOD. WE DON'T NEED THE PIGS LOOKING OUR WAY.
FUCKING SUZY... SHE REALLY DID THAT?
BASHED HIS HEAD IN?
IS THAT A RHETORICAL QUESTION...
OR ARE YOU DOUBTING ME?

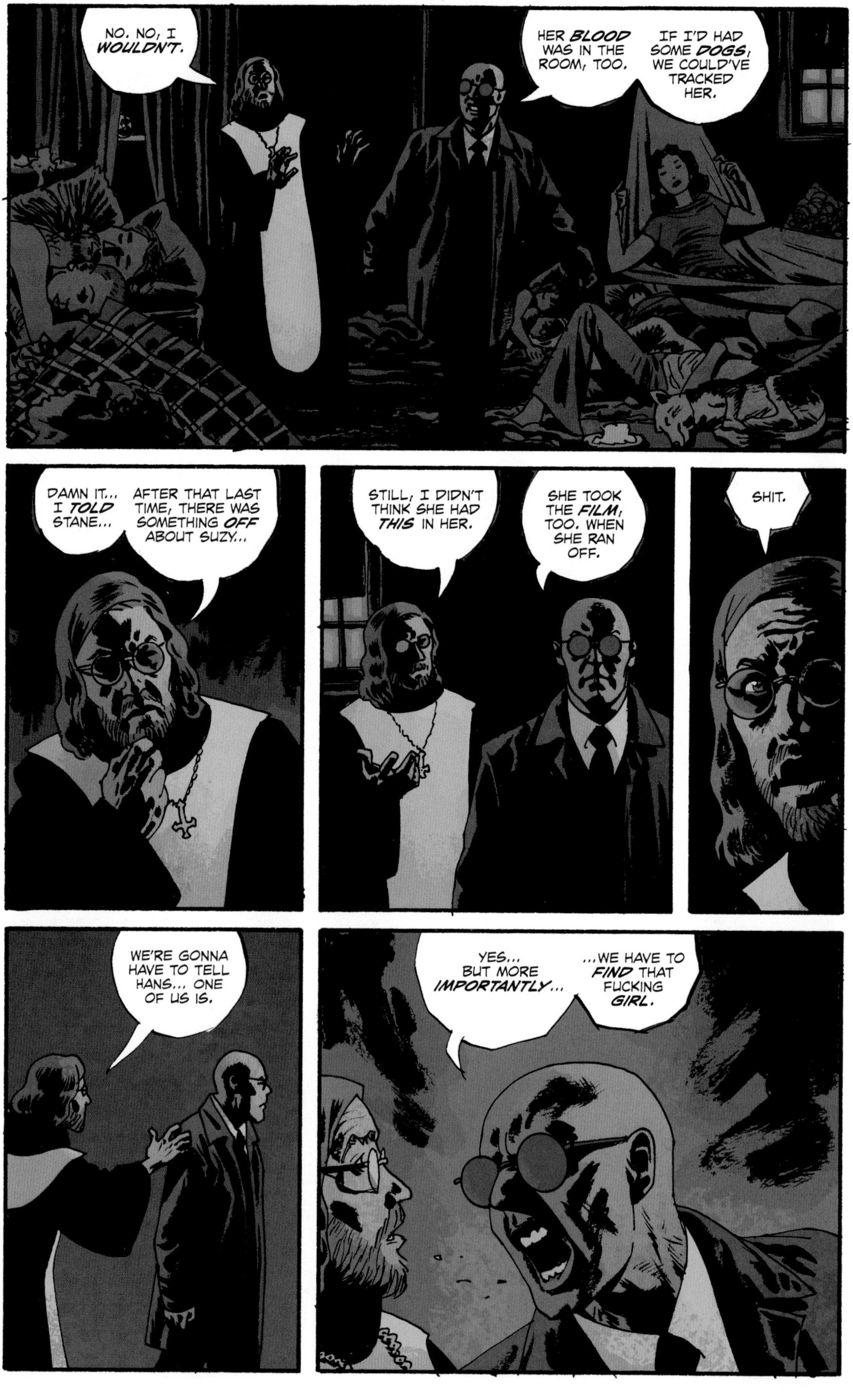
NO. NO, I *WOULDN'T*.
HER *BLOOD* WAS IN THE ROOM, TOO.
IF I'D HAD SOME *DOGS*, WE COULD'VE TRACKED HER.
DAMN IT... I *TOLD* STANE...
AFTER THAT LAST TIME, THERE WAS SOMETHING *OFF* ABOUT SUZY...
STILL, I DIDN'T THINK SHE HAD *THIS* IN HER.
SHE TOOK THE *FILM*, TOO. WHEN SHE RAN OFF.
SHIT.
WE'RE GONNA HAVE TO TELL HANS... ONE OF US IS.
YES... BUT MORE *IMPORTANTLY*...
...WE HAVE TO *FIND* THAT FUCKING *GIRL*.

AHH --!

EASY, GIRLIE...

...DON'T MOVE *TOO* QUICKLY.

WOUND WASN'T *DEEP*, BUT YOU DON'T WANT TO OPEN IT AGAIN.

WHO...?

WAIT -- WHERE AM I?

SOMEPLACE *SAFE.* THAT'S WHERE.

YOU AND YOUR FRIEND ARE *BOTH* SAFE HERE...

FOR THE TIME BEING.

WH... WHERE IS MILES?

HAVING *BREAKFAST* WITH MS. JOSEPHINE...

ALTHOUGH, I CAN'T SEE *WHAT* THEY'D HAVE TO DISCUSS...

BUT I WASN'T *INVITED*... SO WHAT DO I KNOW?

IN FACT, MILES HAD SPENT MOST OF THE MORNING EXPLAINING HOW THEY'D ARRIVED AT JOSEPHINE'S DOORSTEP...

SO ARE YOU GOING TO GIVE ME THE *FILM* BACK, OR NOT?

I HAVEN'T *DECIDED* YET, TO BE HONEST WITH YOU.

I'M NOT SURE I BELIEVE YOU.

HEY, *I'M* NOT THE ONE WHO PICKED SOMEONE'S *POCKETS* HERE.

NO, *YOU'RE* THE ONE WHO RAN STRAIGHT FROM A *DOUBLE-HOMICIDE* TO MY BACK YARD.

I DO *NOT* GET YOU, LADY...

YOU DON'T CALL THE COPS ON US, *EVEN* WHEN YOU LOOK AT THAT FILM REEL...

MOST WOMEN WOULD'A BEEN SCREAMING THEIR *HEADS OFF* IF THEY SAW THAT.

I'VE SEEN *MUCH* WORSE.

BUT IT WASN'T THE *KILLING* THAT INTERESTED ME.

THEN WHAT?

MISS *JOSIE?*

IS EVERYTHING, IT IS *OKAY*?

YES, JORGE... JUST HAVING DISCUSSION WITH A FRIEND.

NOTHING THAT CONCERNS YOU.

MAYBE I JUST *WAIT*? MAKE SURE THIS MAN IS NOT *BOTHERING* YOU?

JORGE HAD BEEN HER GARDENER FOR *YEARS* WITHOUT INCIDENT.

BUT SHE'D LEFT HER CURTAINS OPEN BEFORE AN AFTERNOON *BATH* ONE DAY...

...AND SHE WAS STILL CURSING HERSELF FOR THAT.

NO, YOU WON'T. YOU'LL GO *BACK* TO YOUR WORK. DO YOU HEAR ME?

SI... SI, MISS JOSIE...

WHAT THE HELL WAS *THAT*?

HEY...?

HELLO? WHERE DID YOU GO?

MILES HAD KNOWN TOO MANY *ACTRESSES* TO BE EASILY DRAWN IN BY A MYSTERIOUS WOMAN.

BUT HE COULD ALSO TELL THE DIFFERENCE BETWEEN A REAL MYSTERY...

...AND AN ACT.

THAT'S NOT HANGING FOR A REASON.

WHAT?

OH, SORRY...

FROM TRESPASSING TO *SNOOPING*... WHAT'S A GIRL TO DO?

SO, DID YOU STILL WANT THIS?

YEAH. BUT NOT FOR WHAT YOU THINK.

WHAT I THINK IS THIS THING IS GOING TO GET YOU *KILLED*, BUT THAT'S YOUR BUSINESS.

SO WHY DID YOU WANT TO KNOW ABOUT THE *METHOD CHURCH*, THEN?

THERE WAS A BOOK ONE OF THEM WAS *READING* FROM, BEFORE THE... *SACRIFICE*, I GUESS...

SOME *RELIGIOUS* TOME... SURE...

THEY'RE *CRAZY* FOR THAT SHIT...

WELL, CLEARLY... CRAZY...

LOOKS, UH... LIKE YOU COLLECT THE *SAME* KINDA STUFF...

NO, I *INHERITED* MOST OF THESE.

BUT... YOU *WANT* THE ONE YOU SAW ON THE FILM?

I'M NOT SURE...

...BUT I WANT A BETTER LOOK AT IT...

MILES ALMOST COULDN'T *BELIEVE* HE WAS VOLUNTEERING TO HELP EVEN AS HE HEARD HIMSELF DOING IT...

--SEE WHAT I CAN *FIND OUT*, JUST KEEP AN EYE ON SUZY...

SHE CAN BE A *HANDFUL.*

I'M SURE...

BUT HE'D BEEN MAKING A LOT OF *OUT OF CHARACTER* DECISIONS LATELY.

LIKE NOT *RUNNING* THE SECOND HE SAW SUZY COVERED IN BLOOD AND SCREAMING *IMMINENT DISASTER.*

IF HE WASN'T CAREFUL, HE MIGHT START THINKING HE WAS A *DECENT* HUMAN BEING.

BUT HE KNEW THERE WASN'T *REALLY* MUCH DANGER OF THAT.

YOU NEED SOME *WORKS*, TOO, MAN?

YEAH. YEAH, THANKS.

THE THINGS HE'D *SEEN*, THINGS HE'D *DONE*...

...THAT HE *STILL* REMEMBERED THROUGH THE HAZE...

NO, *"DECENT"* WASN'T A WORD MILES WOULD USE TO DESCRIBE HIMSELF.

AND HE'D NEVER BEEN ASHAMED OF THAT...

...UNTIL THIS MORNING... UNTIL JOSEPHINE...

BUT THE *SPEEDBALL* TAKES CARE OF THE SHAME.

PUTS HIS MIND OFF THE WOMAN AND BACK ON TRACK...

ON HIS WAY OUT.

HE SHOULDN'T HAVE HELPED SUZY... SHOULDN'T HAVE TAKEN THE *FILM* REEL...

WHAT...?

BUT HE HAD.

WHICH WAS A *LESS* OUT OF CHARACTER MOVE...

...BECAUSE HE KNOWS THIS TOWN IS FULL OF MEN WITH STRANGE APPETITES.

POWERFUL MEN, THE KIND WHO COULD MAKE AN ACTOR'S CAREER.

MITCH? *CHRIST...*

THOUGHT YOU WERE *ROOM SERVICE.*

SORRY TO DISAPPOINT...

AND FUCKING STOP *CALLING ME* THAT.

OH FINE, *MILES.*

WHAT THE HELL ARE YOU EVEN *DOING* HERE?

I WAS HOPING TO SEE GAVIN.

CHRIST, MAN, YOU *DON'T* GIVE UP, DO YOU?

GET *FUCKED...*

CLAUDIA CONSTANCE, THE NEXT *IT* GIRL, OR SO THE INDUSTRY RAGS SAID.

OH, POOR MITCHY... SO SENSITIVE.

AND IF THEY SAID IT, IT MUST BE TRUE... THAT WAS THE KIND OF *POWER* GAVIN WILDER HAD.

Claudia On Th Town

SHE'D BEEN JUST PLAIN *CARRIE CONNERS* WHEN THEY WERE STRUGGLING ACTORS FALLING INTO BED, IF NOT LOVE.

THAT WAS BEFORE SHE'D BEEN "DISCOVERED" BY WILDER AND REMADE INTO HIS IMAGE OF A *MOVIE STAR*.

IT AMAZED MILES HOW QUICKLY SHE'D ADAPTED TO FAME AND FORTUNE.

SHE WAS ALREADY BORED OF IT, LIKE SUCCESS HAD ALWAYS JUST BEEN HER DESTINY.

LOOK, I DON'T KNOW WHEN GAVIN'LL BE BACK...

HE'S *LOCATION SCOUTING* WITH FRANCIS AND BOB...

HEY, DO YOU LIKE THIS *BIKINI?*

JESUS... C'MON...

WHAT?

LOOK, I'VE GOT A *MOVIE* YOUR SICK FUCK BOYFRIEND IS GONNA *WANT.*

YOU MADE A MOVIE?

NO. GOD, *NO.* THIS IS MORE LIKE THE ONES IN HIS *PRIVATE* COLLECTION.

WELL... I DON'T KNOW *ANYTHING* ABOUT THAT...

YEAH, YOU'RE *TOTALLY* CLUELESS, I'M SURE...

JUST GIVE HIM THIS. I'LL BE AT THAT NUMBER FOR A WHILE.

TELL HIM IT'S THE *REAL THING.*

FUCKIN' CLAUDIA, HE THOUGHT.

SOME GIRLS LIKED TO RUB *SALT* IN YOUR WOUNDS, SHE PREFERRED *BROKEN GLASS.*

AND SHE *USUALLY* GOT TO HIM. BECAUSE HE WAS JUST AS SCREWED UP AS SHE WAS.

HER SUCCESS YANKED HER OUT OF HIS ORBIT, INTO THE STRATOSPHERE, AND MADE HIS FAILURE EVEN WORSE.

AND HE WAS DISGUSTED BY HOW MUCH THAT MADE HIM *WANT* HER...

USUALLY.

BUT NOT TODAY. WAS HE GETTING *OVER* IT?

HEY, HEY...

...YOU'RE LIKE, *MILES*, RIGHT...?

METHOD CHURCH GIRLS. WHAT THE HELL WERE *THEY* DOING OFF THE COMPOUND?

I'M EM... THIS IS CANDIE...

YOU KNOW *SUZY SCREAM*, RIGHT?

I USED TO, *WHY?*

SHE DIDN'T COME *HOME* LAST NIGHT, AND EVERYONE'S LIKE *WORRIED*...

YEAH, WE'RE ALL OUT TRYING TO *FIND* HER...

SORRY. I HAVEN'T SEEN HER FOR WEEKS...

BUMMER.

WELL, IF YOU *DO* RUN INTO HER, TELL HER ABOUT TONIGHT.

I DON'T *KNOW* ABOUT TONIGHT.

YEAH, *DUH*, CANDIE...

WE'RE HAVING A *MIDNIGHT MASS* AT THE *HOLLYWOOD CEMETERY* FOR BROTHER STANE.

WHAT HAPPENED TO *HIM?*

THEY SAID HE HAD A *HEART ATTACK.*

ANYWAYS, HANSEL *HIMSELF* IS GOING TO LEAD THE CEREMONY.

SUZY *REALLY* SHOULDN'T MISS IT.

OKAY, IF I SEE HER, I'LL GIVE HER THE NEWS.

THANKS...

HE'S TIRED OF WAITING FOR GAVIN WILDER, HE TELLS HIMSELF.

THAT'S WHY HE HURRIES BACK TO JOSEPHINE'S HOUSE.

THE ASSHOLE PROBABLY WASN'T GOING TO CALL ANYWAY...

...MILES? YOU WERE SAYING?

UH, YEAH... SORRY... SORRY...

LOST MY TRAIN OF *THOUGHT*...

ANYWAY, SO THE *METHOD* ARE HAVING SOME KINDA *BLACK MASS* TONIGHT...

A *SEND-OFF* FOR THEIR FALLEN BROTHER ...

MIGHT BE A CHANCE TO GET A LOOK AT THAT *BOOK* YOU'RE SO INTERESTED IN.

WILL *YOU* GO WITH ME?

SURE... YEAH...

SNEAKING AROUND A METHOD CHURCH *CEREMONY* WOULD BE *IMMENSELY* STUPID...

GREAT, I'LL GO GET READY.

...BUT HE KNEW HE'D SAY YES BEFORE SHE EVEN *ASKED*.

ARE YOU *CRAZY?*

I DON'T KNOW.

IF THEY'RE LOOKING FOR *ME*, THEY COULD BE LOOKING FOR *YOU*, TOO.

I DON'T KNOW... SOUNDS LIKE THEY *LIED* TO THE FOLLOWERS...

AND NO ONE REALLY *SAW ME* LAST NIGHT...

I WAS JUST *SOME GUY* WALKIN' THROUGH THEIR ORGY...

EITHER WAY, SHE *CAN'T* GO BY HERSELF.

JESUS, ARE YOU *FUCKING* HER?

WHAT? *NO.* I JUST...

LOOK, SHE'S HELPING US, SO I'M HELPING *HER*, OKAY?

I DON'T LIKE IT, MILES.

I'LL BE *FINE*, OKAY... TRUST ME.

AND HEY, DON'T LET THE *OLD LADY* CATCH YOU WITH THAT *SMACK*, OKAY?

SHE SEEMS PRETTY *UPTIGHT*...

...AN' YOU DON'T WANNA GET *KICKED OUT* OF HERE.

HE WAS RIGHT ABOUT MISS JANSEN. SHE WAS *FURIOUS* JOSEPHINE WAS GOING ON A *SECRET* OUTING...

WARNING HER NOT TO *TRUST* MILES, RIGHT IN *FRONT* OF HIM.

HE COULD ONLY IMAGINE HER REACTION IF SHE SAW *THIS*...

IS THAT *ALL* OF THEM? I DON'T SEE THE *TOME*.

NO... THERE'S A LOT MORE AT THEIR COMPOUND...

DON'T KNOW WHAT THE DEAL IS.

THAT CHICK TOLD ME THEIR *LEADER* WAS GONNA BE HERE...

IT'S NOT THAT GUY IN THE GLASSES?

NAH, THAT'S JUST ONE OF THEIR INNER CIRCLE.

HANSEL'S LIKE... UH... LIKE IF *JAGGER* WAS *JESUS*...

YOU'D KNOW WHAT I *MEAN* IF YOU SAW HIM...

EVEN *MANSON* LISTENED WHEN HANSEL TALKED.

SOUNDS *LOVELY.*

SO, WHAT DO YOU WANNA *DO?*

WAIT AND WATCH THE WHOLE CEREMONY OR *SNEAK OUT?*

I DON'T KNOW.

GOD... I HAVEN'T BEEN HERE IN YEARS.

DON'T THINK I'VE *EVER* BEEN HERE AT NIGHT...

IT'S NICE, ESPECIALLY WITH THE *MOON* LIKE THIS.

YES... IT IS.

HEY, WHERE ARE YOU GOING?

WAIT UP...

SHE WAS GOING TO GET THEM CAUGHT.

HEY!

ANY OTHER GIRL, HE'D HAVE JUST *LEFT* HER THERE, WANDERING THE TOMBSTONES.

AND MILES IS WONDERING WHY HE *ISN'T* DOING THAT...

...WHEN HIS BLOOD RUNS *COMPLETELY COLD.*

DOWN. *NOW.*

WHAT? ARE THERE *MORE?*

JUST SHUT UP AND DON'T MOVE.

DON'T EVEN BREATHE.

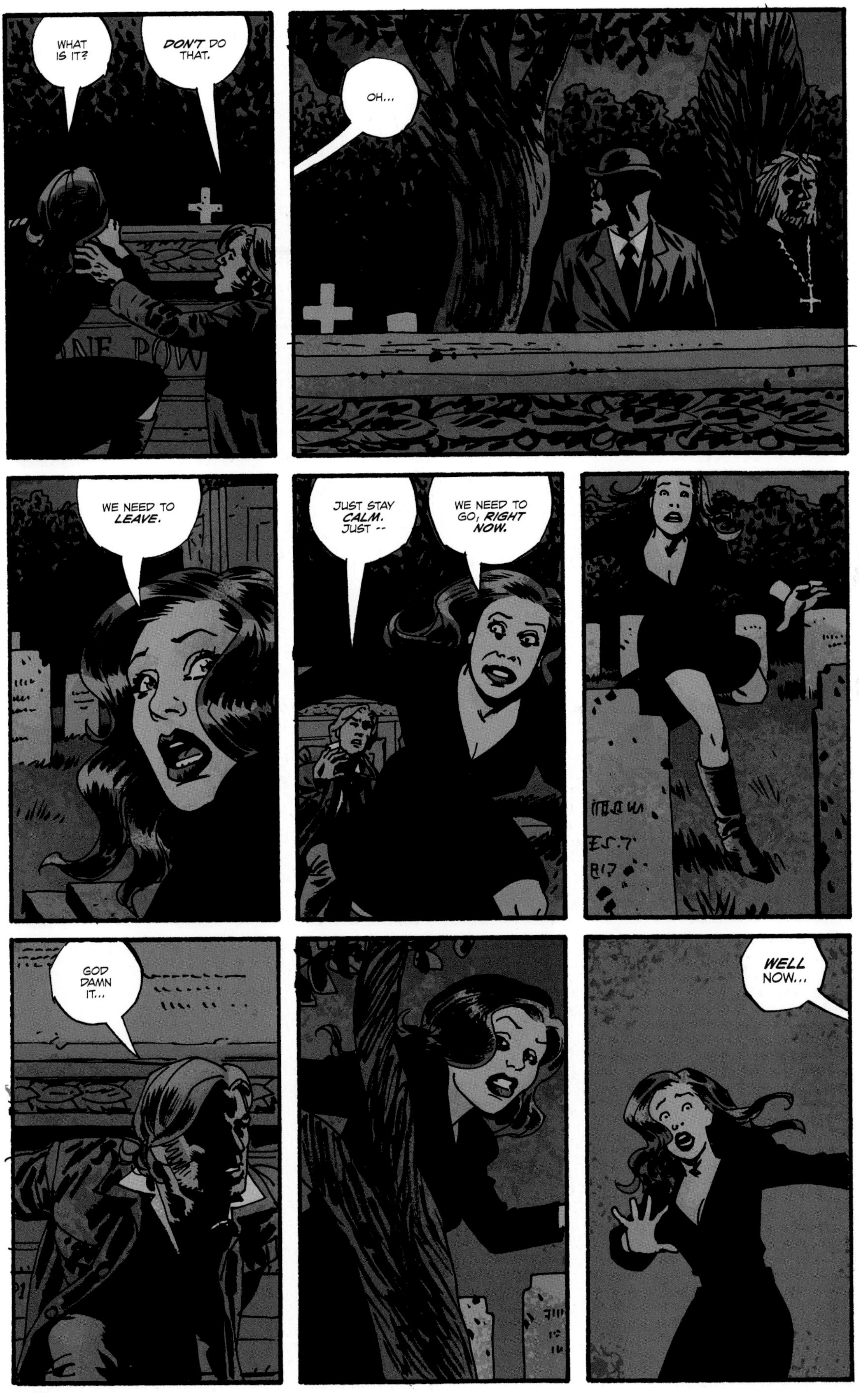
WHAT IS IT?
DON'T DO THAT.
OH...
WE NEED TO *LEAVE.*
JUST STAY *CALM.* JUST --
WE NEED TO GO, *RIGHT NOW.*
GOD DAMN IT...
WELL NOW...

...WHERE DID *YOU* COME FROM?

NO, DON'T ANSWER THAT...

...THE *MASTER* WILL WANT TO ASK *THOSE* QUESTIONS PERSONALLY.

YES... HE'S GOING TO BE *VERY* –

KNNCH

COME ON! WHAT THE HELL ARE YOU JUST *STANDING THERE* FOR?

JOSEPHINE DOESN'T SAY ANYTHING UNTIL THEY'RE FAR AWAY FROM THERE.

UP SOME WINDY STREET OFF *MULHOLLAND*, SOMEWHERE NO ONE EVER GOES.

AND EVEN *THEN*, SHE DOESN'T SAY ANYTHING THAT MAKES ANY *SENSE*...

--IT'S NOT POSSIBLE... THEY'RE ALL DEAD...

JUST CALM DOWN, YOU'RE OKAY...

NO. NO, I'M *NOT*... DON'T YOU *GET IT?*

THEY *SAW* ME.

BUT... THEY DON'T KNOW WHO YOU *ARE*, RIGHT?

SO, YOU'RE *SAFE* NOW...

YOU REALLY DON'T KNOW *ANYTHING*, MILES...

HER LIPS ARE QUIVERING WHEN SHE KISSES HIM, LIKE SHE'S AFRAID.

AND THAT BRINGS *TEARS* TO HIS EYES...

AND HE WONDERS, *WHAT THE HELL IS HAPPENING TO ME?*

HANSEL? ARE YOU AWAKE?

ALWAYS... WHAT IS IT?

SHE'S BEEN *SEEN*...

GAGON SAW HER LAST NIGHT, HE'S CERTAIN OF IT.

GOOD, THEN WE'LL BE GETTING OUR *FILM* BACK.

AND WE CAN FIND A NEW BUYER.

IS *THAT* SO...?

NO, NO... NOT SUZY, MASTER. FORGIVE ME.

I MEANT *THE CONSORT.*

SHE'S *HERE*, IN LOS ANGELES.

Interlude

Since the incident in *Santa Barbara*, I hadn't slept in the same place more than a few nights at a time.

It turns out that even in our high-speed wired world...

...you can still drop off the grid, with a bit of *effort.*

And a bit more *cash.*

More than I could *afford*, really.

But after I saw the empty eyes of the *Freak* who'd been *following* me, all I could do was run.

Because *fear* is a great motivator.

But I didn't have a plan, and after two months on the road... I was worn out.

Maybe that's why it happened, because of exhaustion.

Or maybe it was *Jo*, playing with my head from afar.

All I know is, I *saw* something...

...And it was like a *door* ripping open in my mind.

Some forgotten *childhood memory*... suddenly *unlocked*.

Me and my Dad and *Dominic* are on a road trip to Los Angeles.

I'm six or seven... so it has to be the *late 70s*.

I don't remember much... just a few images... a few fragments...

We're visiting a *woman*.

I watch cartoons while the adults talk.

Dominic's warning her about some *men* he saw in San Francisco.

He's upset, angry... and she tries to calm him.

Later, when we're *leaving*, she stops my Dad...

...and says something to him...

And she sees me listening.

HEY, NICK... YOU KNOW HOW TO KEEP A *SECRET*, DON'T YOU?

On the way home, Dominic breaks down.

I'm asleep by then, already dreaming of the pretty lady who broke his heart...

But when I wake up, I don't think about her again...

And I *don't* recognize her when I see her at Dominic's funeral.

MOTHERFUCK ME...

EXCUSE ME?

OH, SORRY... I WASN'T...

I WAS JUST... TALKING TO MYSELF.

UH HUNH... STRANGE MAN, DRINKING ALONE AND MUTTERING TO HIMSELF.

YOU'RE EITHER INTERESTING ... OR A PSYCHO.

SO, WHICH IS IT?

I guess she picks *interesting*... Although she doesn't actually say.

I'm too distracted to wonder about it, really...

Realizing I haven't even *thought* about another woman since I met Jo...

Wondering if she's been hiding in my *subconscious* all my life...

And *that's* why none of my relationships ever worked out...

... I DOIN' SOMETHIN' *WRONG*, BABY...?

NO...NO... I'M JUST... TOO DRUNK, I THINK...

Because secretly I was always waiting for her...

And I didn't even know it.

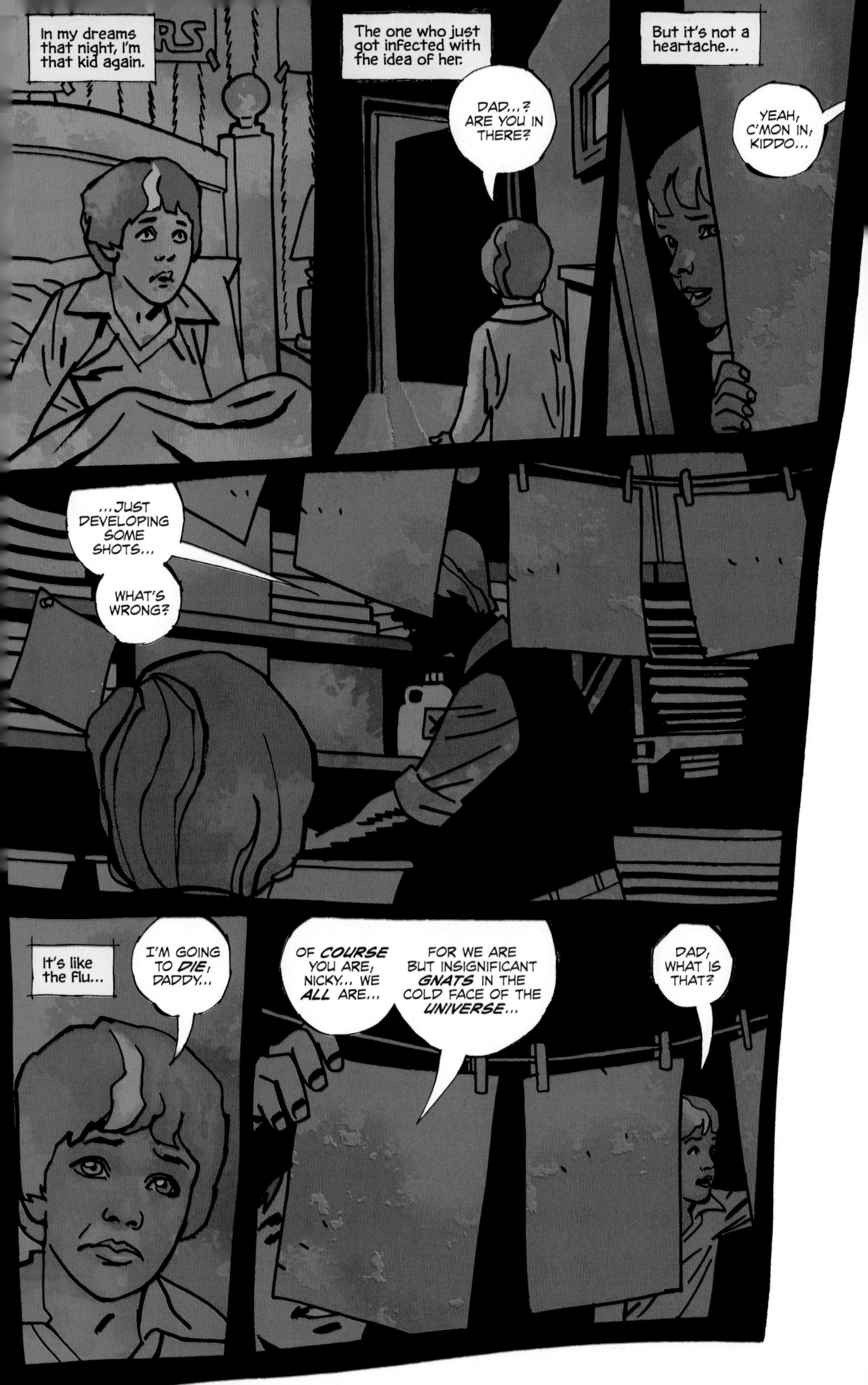
In my dreams that night, I'm that kid again.
The one who just got infected with the idea of her.
DAD...? ARE YOU IN THERE?
But it's not a heartache...
YEAH, C'MON IN, KIDDO...
...JUST DEVELOPING SOME SHOTS...
WHAT'S WRONG?
It's like the flu...
I'M GOING TO *DIE*, DADDY...
OF *COURSE* YOU ARE, NICKY... WE *ALL* ARE...
FOR WE ARE BUT INSIGNIFICANT *GNATS* IN THE COLD FACE OF THE *UNIVERSE*...
DAD, WHAT IS THAT?

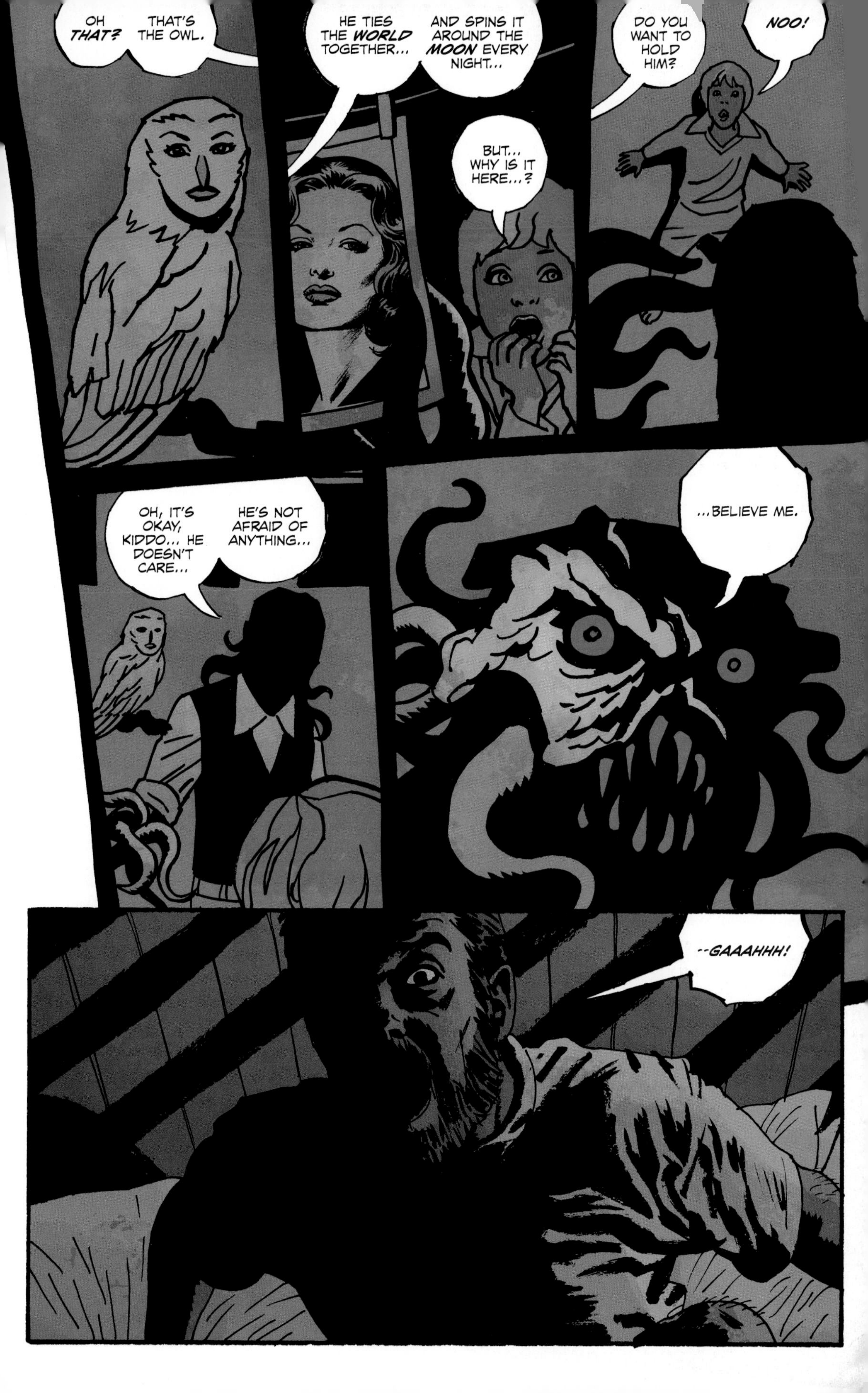
OH THAT?
THAT'S THE OWL.
HE TIES THE WORLD TOGETHER...
AND SPINS IT AROUND THE MOON EVERY NIGHT...
BUT... WHY IS IT HERE...?
DO YOU WANT TO HOLD HIM?
NOO!
OH, IT'S OKAY, KIDDO... HE DOESN'T CARE...
HE'S NOT AFRAID OF ANYTHING...
...BELIEVE ME.
--GAAAHHH!

When I calm down enough to think...

I realize there was something *in* that nightmare...

Some kind of *clue* to my Josephine mystery...

WHERE IS IT...? WHERE IS IT...?

WHERE THE HELL IS IT...?

That *folk tale* about the owl and the ribbon, it was in Dominic's unpublished manuscript.

And I think I'm finally about to *understand* whatever it means...

...When I notice the *girl* isn't in my bed anymore.

HEY... WHAT'S THAT --

-- ABOUT?

RRRRAAAA --

KRAAAK

Do I even have to tell you the rest?

That when I wake up a few hours later...

...FUUUCKKK...

...Everything, even that *manuscript*, is gone.

Chapter Three

THERE HAD BEEN STORMY SKIES EVERY NIGHT THAT WEEK.

EVER SINCE SHE'D BEEN *SEEN*, SHE THINKS.

LIKE THE WORLD ITSELF IS MAD AT HER, FOR HER STUPIDITY.

OR LIKE IT'S LAUGHING...

...BECAUSE SHE JUST KEEPS MAKING THE SAME MISTAKES OVER AND OVER.

SHE'S ASHAMED OF HERSELF, FOR THINKING SHE HAD CHANGED.

BUT SHE WAS JUST HIDING... AND NOW THE DARK PLACES KNEW.

AND THEY WERE ALREADY REACHING OUT, SEARCHING FOR HER.

HANK'S *VISIT* TODAY CONFIRMED THAT, IF SHE HAD ANY DOUBTS...

SORRY TO JUST *SHOW UP* LIKE THIS...

I KNOW. I KNOW I'M NOT... SUPPOSED TO...

IT HAD BEEN NEARLY TWENTY YEARS SINCE SHE'D SEEN HIM...

NONSENSE, PLEASE, COME IN... ALL OF YOU.

...AND IT MUST HAVE BEEN NEARLY IMPOSSIBLE FOR HIM MAKE THIS JOURNEY.

--THEY WERE IN MY *BUILDING*, DO YOU UNDERSTAND?

THEY COULDN'T GET PAST THE *OBSTRUCTION*... COULDN'T GET TO ME...

BUT... YOU AREN'T *SAFE* ANYMORE, JO.

ARE *YOU?*

DO YOU HAVE ANOTHER PLACE TO GO?

YEAH, I HAVE A HOUSE THEY CAN'T *GET* TO... OUT IN THE WOODS.

THEN GO THERE, AND *DON'T* LEAVE... ...NOT UNTIL YOU HEAR FROM ME.

IT TORE PIECES OUT OF HER TO SEE HIM LIKE THAT...

AGING... FRAGILE... SCARED...

SHE COULDN'T RUIN HIS LIFE AGAIN...

SHE COULDN'T BEAR THAT.

SHE'D BEEN SO SCARED AFTER THAT NIGHT IN THE CEMETERY...

CLINGING TO MILES... HIDING IN HIS ARMS...

THINKING, AT LEAST THIS ONE DOESN'T HAVE A LIFE *TO* RUIN.

BUT SHE FELT *ALIVE* AGAIN, TOO, IN HIS PASSION.

AN UNINTENDED SIDE EFFECT, BUT IT WAS THERE... THAT SPARK.

AND NOW HANK HAD BROUGHT BACK EVERYTHING *ELSE* SHE'D BEEN TRYING TO FORGET...

NOT JUST THE MEN WHO FOLLOWED THE MONSTER...

HEY...

...WHAT'RE YOU *DOING?* IT'S RAINING...

JUST THINKING.

AND THERE'S A FIRE STARTING INSIDE HER, SHE THINKS.

WELL, COME BACK TO BED... *I'M* AWAKE AGAIN, TOO.

SHE'S TIRED OF BEING AFRAID...

YOU'RE OUT OF YOUR MIND...

PROBABLY.

TIRED OF HIDING...

HEY, WHY DID I HAVE TO STAY UP HERE WHEN THAT *OLD GUY* CAME OVER?

OH... DON'T *START,* MILES...

...JUST BE HAPPY WITH WHAT YOU'VE GOT.

TIRED OF MEMORIES...

...AND TIRED OF RUNNING FROM THIS GODDAMN STORM.

IF HE COULD *SEE* HIS HANDIWORK, HANSEL WOULD BE SMILING.

INSTEAD, HE WAS THINKING ABOUT WHICH SERVANT TO *SACRIFICE* NEXT.

AND WONDERING HOW MANY MORE HE COULD *AFFORD* TO LOSE...

...WITH NO RESULT.

HE CURSES HIMSELF *AGAIN* FOR HIS GREED...

AND FOR UNDERESTIMATING THE WOMAN'S *EFFECT* ON HER VICTIMS...

THAT FAT COP *BASTARD* HAD TAKEN MORE THAN JUST HIS *EYES* THAT DAY...

HE'D TAKEN AWAY HIS ONLY CONNECTION TO THE *TRUE* WORLD...

WHERE HIS FATHERS LIVED...

FOR TWENTY YEARS HE'D BEEN TRAPPED IN THIS PRISON...

UNABLE TO FEEL THE COLD TOUCH OF THE UNIVERSE INSIDE HIM...

UNABLE TO READ HIS MASTER'S NAME SCRAWLED ACROSS THE SKY...

AND UNABLE TO SEE THE WOMAN, OR SENSE HER PRESENCE...

HE'D TAKEN WHAT PLEASURE HE COULD IN THOSE YEARS...

AND DONE HIS DUTY TO HIS PATRONS...

BUT EVEN MANIPULATING THESE PEASANTS INTO INSANITY AND MURDER...

IT WAS AN EMPTY PLEASURE.

BUT HE KNEW THE UNIVERSE WELL, AND NOTHING THE DEMON GODS HAD TOUCHED...

...WAS EVER TRULY FREE OF THEIR GRASP.

AND SOON HE'D *HAVE* HER...

AND HE'D KNOW THAT *TOUCH* AGAIN.

THIS FEELS *AMAZING*... YOU SHOULD COME IN...

JUST GET YOUR *FEET* WET.

I'M *OKAY* HERE... AND I'VE GOT THE BEST VIEW.

HE FELT SICK SAYING *NO* TO HER, EVEN FOR SOMETHING THAT SMALL...

...BUT MILES COULDN'T *SWIM*, AND DIDN'T WANT TO ADMIT IT.

HEY, WE'RE GONNA BE *LATE*, BABE.

HE COULDN'T BEAR THE IDEA OF LOOKING *WEAK* IN JOSEPHINE'S EYES.

SO... THE METHOD CHURCH WAS *SELLING* THAT FILM REEL YOU STOLE?

YEAH, AND FOR *A LOT*, I'M GUESSIN'.

THAT'S A *BIG PART* OF WHAT THEY DO...

SELLIN' SICK *SHIT* TO RICH *FUCKS*.

AND YOUR FRIEND SUZY... IS SHE THE *OTHER PART* OF WHAT THEY DO?

YEAH... BUT LOOK, DON'T BLAME SUZE.

SHE'S A GOOD KID. JUST LIKED TO PARTY TOO MUCH...

THEN SHE SAW HANSEL TALKIN'... AN' IT WAS LIKE, SHE COULDN'T HEAR ANYONE ELSE AFTER THAT...

NOT FOR A *WHILE*, AT LEAST...

WHAT AREN'T YOU *SAYING*, MILES?

I *LEFT HER* THERE... *OKAY*?

SAW HER *GAZING* AT THIS GUY LIKE SHE WAS IN FUCKIN' *LOVE*...

AN' I JUST *BAILED*... THOUGHT, FUCK HER...

NEXT TIME I SEE HER, SHE'S STRUNG OUT AN' RUNNIN' WITH THE OTHER METHOD CHICKS...

SUCKIN' OFF *OLD MEN* WHO DONATE TO HANSEL'S *CAUSE*.

YOU KNOW THAT'S NOT YOUR FAULT.

I DON'T KNOW *WHAT* I KNOW...

HERE... THIS WAY...

JUST STICK *CLOSE* TO ME...

THIS *ISN'T* THE WORLD'S GREATEST NEIGHBORHOOD.

IT'S NOT *THAT* BAD, MILES... I'M NOT SOME SPOILED LITTLE RICH GIRL.

--THE FUCK *OUT!!*

HEY!

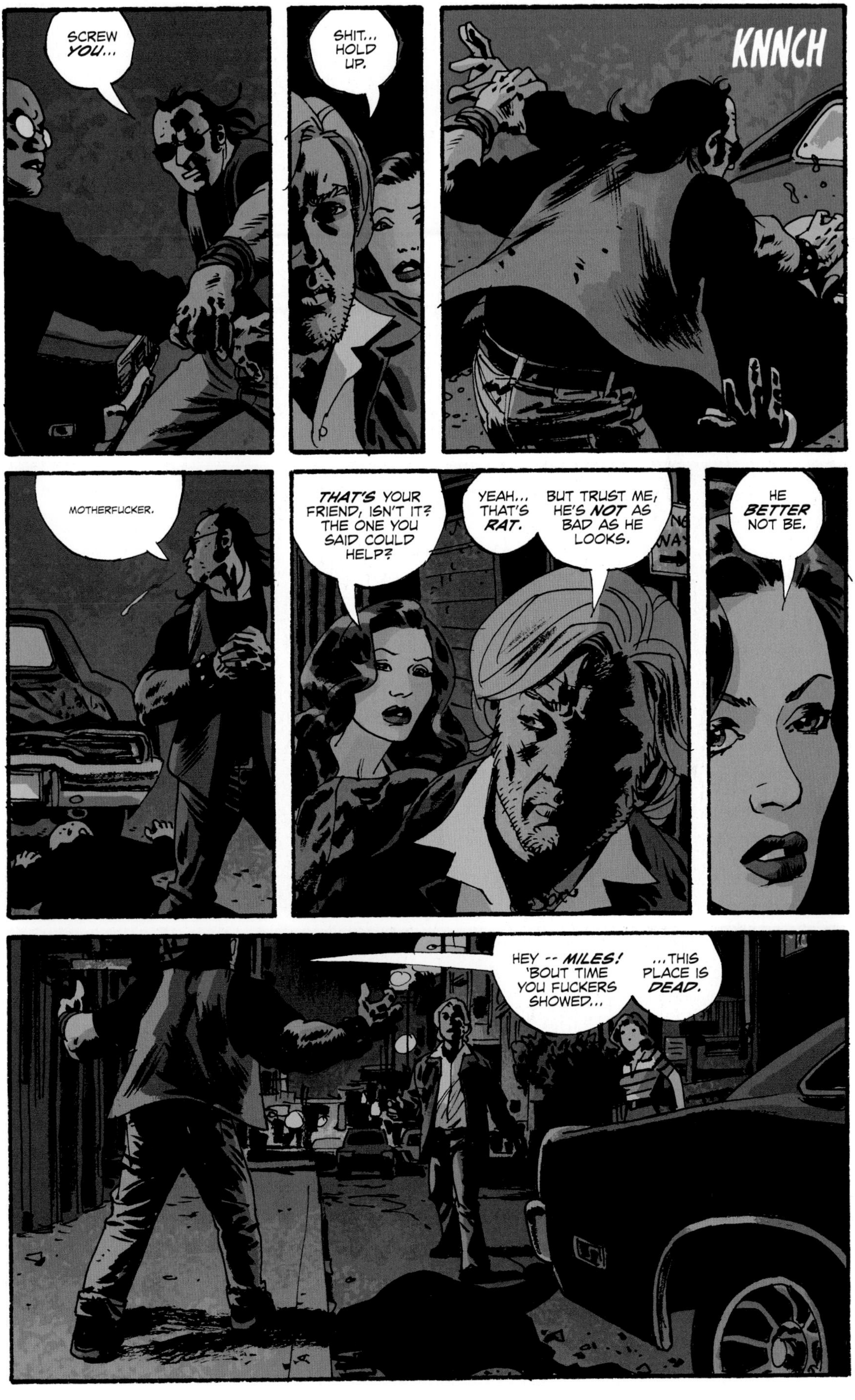

SCREW YOU...
SHIT... HOLD UP.
KNNCH
MOTHERFUCKER.
THAT'S YOUR FRIEND, ISN'T IT? THE ONE YOU SAID COULD HELP?
YEAH... THAT'S RAT.
BUT TRUST ME, HE'S NOT AS BAD AS HE LOOKS.
HE BETTER NOT BE.
HEY -- MILES! 'BOUT TIME YOU FUCKERS SHOWED...
...THIS PLACE IS DEAD.

THIS WHOLE HOUSE JUST FELT *WRONG*, SUZY THOUGHT.

GAVE OFF UGLY *VIBES*... LIKE SOME NIGHTMARE...

BUT SHE WAS THE ONLY ONE WHO COULD FEEL IT.

AND THAT *JOSEPHINE*...

SHE WAS THE ONLY ONE WHO COULD TELL SOMETHING WAS OFF ABOUT *HER*, TOO.

NO ONE WHO LOOKED LIKE THAT LIVED ALONE IN A BIG EMPTY NIGHTMARE HOUSE.

LIKE *"WHATEVER HAPPENED TO BABY JANE?"*

OR NORMA DESMOND...

HIDING FROM YOUR MYSTERIOUS PAST... THAT'S WHAT *OLD LADIES* DID...

COP DIES SOLVING MURDER

The San Francisco Gazette

NOT —

WAIT... WAIT...

JESUS -- THAT'S – THAT --

OH FUCK...

HELLO? IS SOMEBODY IN HERE?

SINCE JOINING THE CHURCH, SUZY HAD SEEN THINGS MOST PEOPLE WOULDN'T BELIEVE...

EVEN IF THEY WERE *CAPABLE* OF SEEING THEM.

AND SHE KNEW -- SHE *ALWAYS* KNEW -- IT WASN'T JUST THE DRUGS...

BUT SHE'D NEVER SEEN ANYONE LIKE THAT... WHO STAYED YOUNG FOREVER...

WHAT THE HELL *WAS* THIS WOMAN?

FUCK... FUCK FUCK FUCK...

SOME KIND OF DEMON?

HEY, *SUZY SCREAM*... WE'VE BEEN LOOKING EVERYWHERE FOR YOU.

WHA - WAIT - WAIT -

GET IN THE FUCKING *CAR*, SUZY...

Chapter Four

SHE HAD KNOWN FOR A WHILE THAT THIS IS HOW IT WOULD END...

--THE HELL WERE YOU THINKIN', SUZY?

...THAT THESE PEOPLE SHE'D LOVED WOULD BE THE ONES WHO KILLED HER.

THINK YOU COULD DO WHAT YOU *DID* AND JUST... JUST... *RUN AWAY?*

FROM *US?*

KNOWN IT IN THAT WAY YOU DON'T WANT TO ADMIT, EVEN TO YOURSELF.

THINK WE'D JUST LET THAT GO?

BUT THAT HAD BEEN THE TRAJECTORY OF HER LIFE...

NUH UH, BABY... NO WAY...

...GIVING HER LOVE TO ALL THE WRONG MEN AND BEING PUNISHED FOR IT.

...*SUUUZZY*... DADDY'S GOT A *PREZZIE* FOR YOU...

HANSEL HAD BEEN DIFFERENT AT FIRST. HIS TOUCH AND HIS VOICE WERE LIKE MAGIC...

BUT HE WANTED EVERYONE *ELSE* TO TOUCH HER, TOO.

SOLD HER TO CREEPS AND POLITICIANS AND OLD MEN...

UNTIL SHE'D SHOWED THEM HOW BROKEN SHE *REALLY* WAS...

AFTER THAT, SHE KNEW IT WAS JUST A MATTER OF TIME.

MAYBE THAT'S WHY SHE'D KILLED BROTHER STANE, NOT *JUST* BECAUSE OF THAT FILM...

MAYBE SHE WAS SICK OF *WAITING*...

AND THEN *MILES* HAD SHOWED UP AND RUINED IT ALL.

HEY - !

KRAAK

AT LEAST SHE CAN PROTECT *HIM*, SHE THINKS...

BECAUSE SHE KNOWS SHE *WON'T* BE ABLE TO LIE TO HANSEL...

EVEN THOUGH HE'S A *MONSTER*...

...LIKE ALL THE *OTHERS* SHE'S LOVED.

SHIT... FUCKIN' HELL...

WELL, DON'T JUST FUCKING STAND THERE, MAN...

PICK HER UP... SOMEONE MIGHTA *HEARD* THAT...

SOUNDS LIKE A *BLAST*, MAN.

LIKE BEIN' BACK IN THE *FUCKIN'* JUNGLE.

RAT TALKED ABOUT *WAM* LIKE IT WAS SOME CHAMPIONSHIP GAME FROM HIGH SCHOOL...

...WHICH HAD ALWAYS FREAKED MILES OUT A BIT.

CHRIST, I *HOPE* NOT.

LEAVE IT TO A *STUNTMAN* TO MISS BEING AT *WAR*.

WHAT KINDA WEAPONS ARE WE LOOKIN' AT?

PROBABLY *HATCHETS*, KNIVES...

MAYBE A *SHOTGUN* OR TWO.

RIGHT... GOOD...

BUT THAT KIND OF CRAZINESS WAS WHAT THEY NEEDED, IF THEY WERE GOING TO INFILTRATE THE METHOD CHURCH'S *COMPOUND*.

PRETTY SURE I CAN PICK US UP SOME *AK'S*... WHAT'S OUR TIME FRAME?

SOON... THE NEXT FEW *DAYS* WOULD BE BEST.

DAMN, LADY... I LIKE YOUR *STYLE.*

BACK OFF, RAT...

JUST MAKIN' A COMPLIMENT...

BUT YOU EVER GET SICK'A *NEEDLE-DICK* HERE, YOU GIMME A SHOUT.

CAN WE JUST STICK TO THE *SUBJECT,* BOYS?

SUZY WOULD BE THE KEY TO THEIR SUCCESS.

THE METHOD WERE SCOURING THE CITY FOR HER.

SO A QUICK *SIGHTING* DOWNTOWN WOULD GET RID OF MOST OF THE COMPOUND'S BIGGEST THREATS...

...LEAVING AN EASY PATH FOR MILES AND RAT TO THE CHURCH'S *INNER SANCTUM.*

JOSEPHINE FELT HAPPY AND SCARED AT THE SAME TIME...

INSTEAD OF RUNNING AWAY FROM TROUBLE, NOW SHE WAS RUNNING TOWARDS IT.

BUT SHE WAS TAKING CONTROL. *ACTING* INSTEAD OF *REACTING*.

AND SHE HADN'T FELT LIKE THIS IN A LONG TIME... POWERFUL...

PRACTICALLY VIBRATING WITH POTENTIAL.

SHE AND MILES MAKE LOVE THAT NIGHT UNTIL THEY PASS OUT.

IT'S LIKE NOTHING EXISTS OUTSIDE THAT BEDROOM.

AT LEAST UNTIL MORNING...

GONE?! WHAT THE HELL DO YOU MEAN?

IT ISN'T MY FAULT...

I WENT TO CHECK ON HER AND HER BED WAS EMPTY...

SHE RAN OFF.

YOU WERE SUPPOSED TO BE TAKING CARE OF HER!

AND YOU JUST LET HER—

MILES, EASE UP.

DO YOU UNDERSTAND WHAT'S GONNA HAPPEN IF THEY FIND HER?

YES... BETTER THAN YOU DO, I'M SURE.

GOOD RIDDANCE TO BAD *RUBBISH,* I SAY.

WHAT?

SHE WAS A *DRUGGIE.* THINK I DON'T *KNOW?*

CREEPING AROUND, *SNOOPING...*

LOOKING FOR WHAT TO *STEAL* FROM MS JOSEPHINE...

LADY, GET OUTTA MY FACE OR I'M GONNA *HURT* YOU.

MILES!

FUCKING BITCH PROBABLY THREW HER OUT...

SHE *WOULDN'T* DO THAT...

...SHE *LISTENS* TO ME...

YEAH... WELL, TOO BAD YOU NEVER TALKED TO SUZY...

MILES KNOWS HE'S NOT GOING TO FIND HER, BUT HE KEEPS LOOKING ANYWAY...

ALL HER OLD HANGOUTS...

THE PLACES SHE MIGHT TRY TO SCORE...

HE CRISS-CROSSES L.A. FROM HOLLYWOOD TO THE BEACHES...

MOVING FROM ANGRY TO FRANTIC TO RESIGNED...

HE PRAYS SHE STOLE SOME *MONEY* FROM JO'S HOUSE... GOT ON A BUS OUT OF TOWN...

BUT HE *KNOWS* SUZY... KNOWS IT'S JUST AS LIKELY SHE RAN RIGHT BACK TO THE *METHOD* COMPOUND...

...CRAZY FUCKING GIRL...

CLAUDIA?

WHAT'RE YOU DOIN' HERE?

HOPING THIS WAS STILL WHERE YOU *LIVED*, MOSTLY...

GAVIN WANTED ME TO *INVITE* YOU TO *HIS PLACE* TONIGHT.

THERE'S A PARTY.

REALLY? *I'M* INVITED TO A *GAVIN WILDER* PARTY?

Miles

TURNS OUT HE IS INTERESTED IN THIS *MOVIE* YOU WANNA SELL...

I FORGOT TO TELL HIM ABOUT IT UNTIL YESTERDAY...

HE WAS *PISSED*.

JESUS...

YEAH, I MENTIONED HIS *PRIVATE COLLECTION* THE WAY YOU DID...

AND HE WAS ALL *"HOW THE FUCK COULD YOU LET HIM GO?"*

THE FUCKER *HIT* YOU?

IT'S NO BIG DEAL... HE'S *OLD...* DOESN'T HIT THAT HARD.

SO, WHAT'RE YOU UP TO NOW?

NOTHING... JUST ERRANDS.

WANNA COME GET A DRINK? I'VE GOT SOME GOOD *COKE* IN THE LIMO.

NAH... I'VE STILL GOT THINGS TO DO.

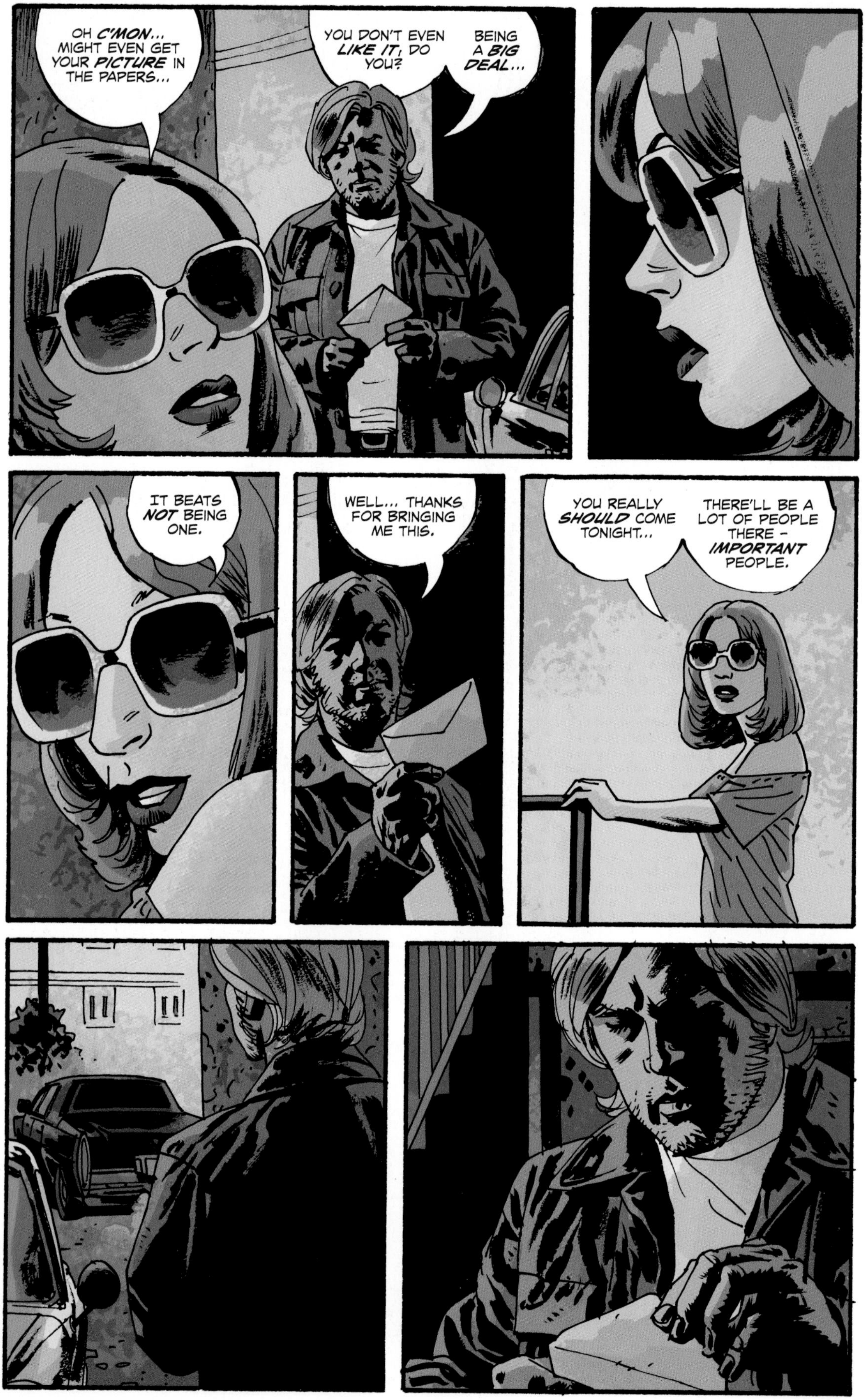
OH *C'MON*... MIGHT EVEN GET YOUR *PICTURE* IN THE PAPERS...
YOU DON'T EVEN *LIKE IT*, DO YOU?
BEING A *BIG DEAL*...
IT BEATS *NOT* BEING ONE.
WELL... THANKS FOR BRINGING ME THIS.
YOU REALLY *SHOULD* COME TONIGHT...
THERE'LL BE A LOT OF PEOPLE THERE – *IMPORTANT* PEOPLE.

IT'S ONLY AFTER CLAUDIA LEAVES AND MILES REALIZES HE FEELS *SORRY* FOR HER...

THAT HE HAS A MOMENT OF *CLARITY*...

...ABOUT HOW MUCH HE'S *CHANGED* IN THE PAST WEEK.

HE HASN'T USED ANYTHING BUT *POT* SINCE HE FIRST SLEPT WITH JOSEPHINE.

AND HE HASN'T EVEN MISSED IT. NO CRAVINGS... NOTHING.

LIKE SHE WAS ALL THE DRUGS HE NEEDED.

AND NOW HE WAS PREPARING TO THROW AWAY HIS *LAST CHANCE*... ALL TO HELP HER.

BECAUSE THEY NEEDED A *NEW DISTRACTION* TO LURE THE METHOD...

AND *THAT'S* WHAT CLAUDIA HAD JUST DROPPED INTO HIS LAP.

FOR ONE BRIEF MOMENT, HE TRIES TO UNDERSTAND WHAT'S HAPPENING TO HIM...

TRIES TO THINK ABOUT POOR SUZY, LOST OUT THERE AGAIN, OR WORSE...

BUT HE'S LIKE A DROWNING MAN BURSTING THROUGH THE SURFACE ONE LAST TIME...

...BEFORE BEING SUCKED BACK UNDER.

THE ONLY THING THAT *STICKS* IN HIS MIND ANYMORE IS *JO*.

YOU'RE *ABSOLUTELY* SURE? IT'S *HER*?

YES, NO QUESTION... TAKEN SOME TIME IN THE '30S.

SUZY SCREAM HAD *THAT* PHOTO ON HER...

...AND YOU *KILLED HER* BEFORE *BRINGING HER* TO ME?

B – BUT – IT WASN'T LIKE THAT, HANS... SHE – SHE –

HIS PRAYERS WERE BEING *HEARD*, HANSEL THOUGHT. *FINALLY.*

SUZY WAS BEING DRAWN *BACK* TO HIM, TO SHOW HIM THE WAY TO FIND HIS PREY.

AND THIS FOOL, HIS *OWN* MAN...

HANSEL, PLEASE... LISTEN, WAIT – LISTEN TO –

...HAD *DENIED HIM* THE GIFT OF HIS GODS.

UKK -- !

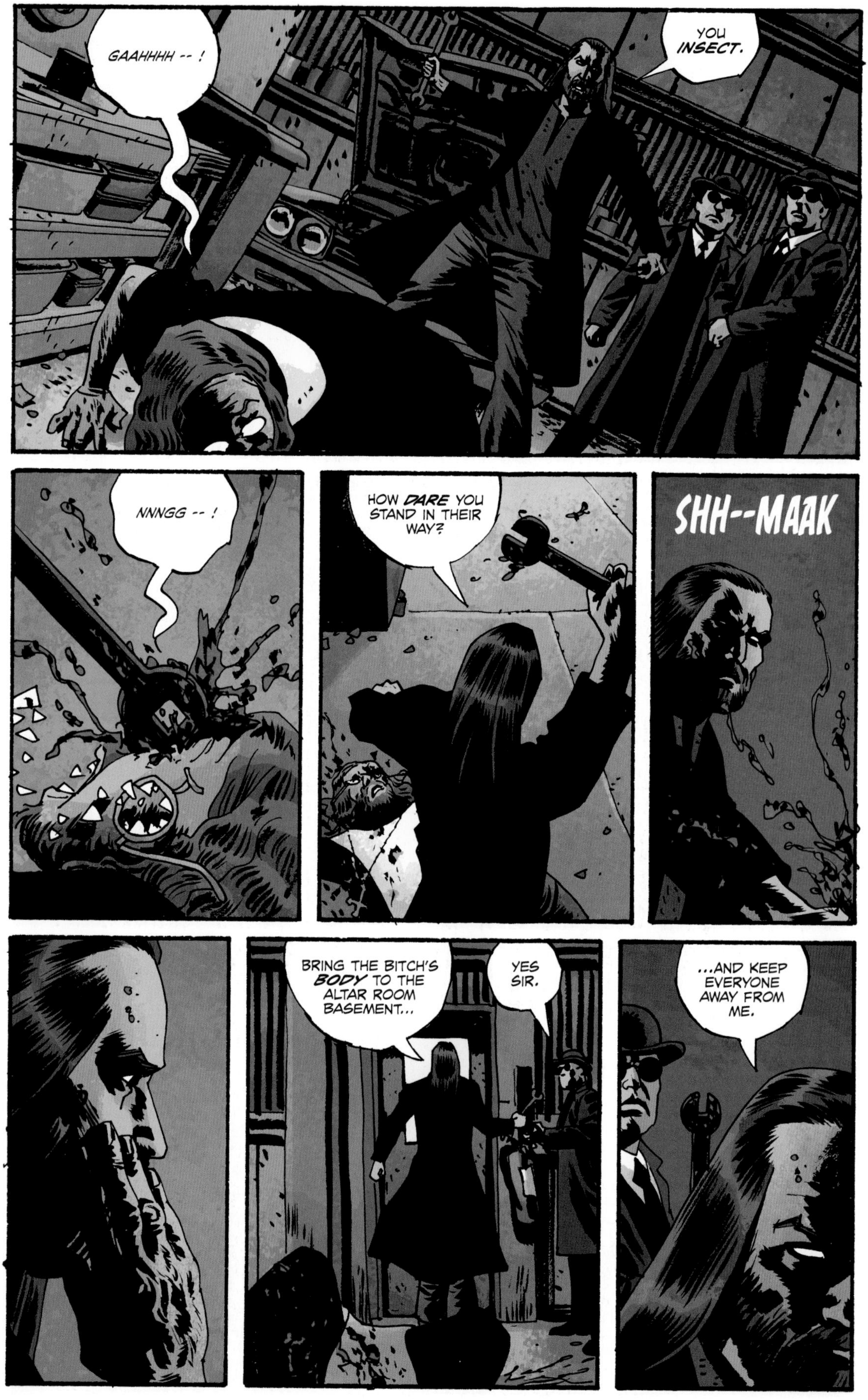
GAAHHHH -- !
YOU INSECT.
NNNGG -- !
HOW DARE YOU STAND IN THEIR WAY?
SHH--MAAK
BRING THE BITCH'S BODY TO THE ALTAR ROOM BASEMENT...
YES SIR.
...AND KEEP EVERYONE AWAY FROM ME.

THERE WAS STILL *ONE THING* THAT WAS BUGGING HIM...

WHAT MISS JANSEN HAD SAID ABOUT HOW SUZY WAS ALWAYS "SNOOPING."

MILES DIDN'T DOUBT THAT FOR A SECOND.

NO, HIS QUESTION WAS...

WHAT...? A *KID*?

...WHAT HAD SHE *FOUND*?

MILES? ARE YOU *READY*?

COMING!

I FORGET HOW LATE IS *FASHIONABLE* IN THIS TOWN... BUT I THINK WE'RE *PAST* IT.

MY GOD... YOU LOOK AMAZING.

THANKS. I HAVEN'T BEEN TO A PARTY IN... WELL, A *LONG* TIME.

AND IT WAS SAFE TO SAY SHE'D *NEVER* BEEN TO A PARTY LIKE ONE OF GAVIN WILDER'S...

IT WAS ONE OF THOSE *"EVERYONE WHO'S ANYONE"* KIND OF AFFAIRS SHE USUALLY JUST READ ABOUT IN THE PAPERS.

HOLLYWOOD *ROYALTY* AND ALL THAT CAME WITH THEM.

MILES SHOULD BE IN HIS ELEMENT HERE. THIS WAS HIS WORLD, OR AT LEAST WHAT HIS WORLD *ORBITED.*

BUT THE WHOLE RIDE OVER, HE'D BEEN DISTRACTED AND QUIET.

SHE ALMOST THINKS, *NOT HIMSELF...* BUT THEN, SHE WOULDN'T REALLY KNOW.

WHAT IS IT? ARE YOU WORRYING ABOUT *SUZY?*

WHAT?

NO... I MEAN, I *SHOULD* BE... BUT...

AND JOSEPHINE HATES HERSELF SO MUCH RIGHT THEN.

SHE'S SEEN THAT LOOK SO MANY TIMES... THAT CONFUSION... THAT STRUGGLE...

ONLY *THIS* TIME, SOMETHING'S DIFFERENT...

WHO'S THE LITTLE BOY... IN THE *PICTURE* WITH YOU?

WHAT? MILES, WHAT DID YOU...?

I KNOW, I SHOULDN'T HAVE... SORRY...

THAT'S MY SON.

WELL... WHY ARE YOU –

MILES?

YOU ARE *MILES*, RIGHT?

UH, *YEAH...?*

GREAT... YOU LOOK JUST LIKE YOUR *HEADSHOT*. GAVIN'S BEEN *WAITING* FOR YOU.

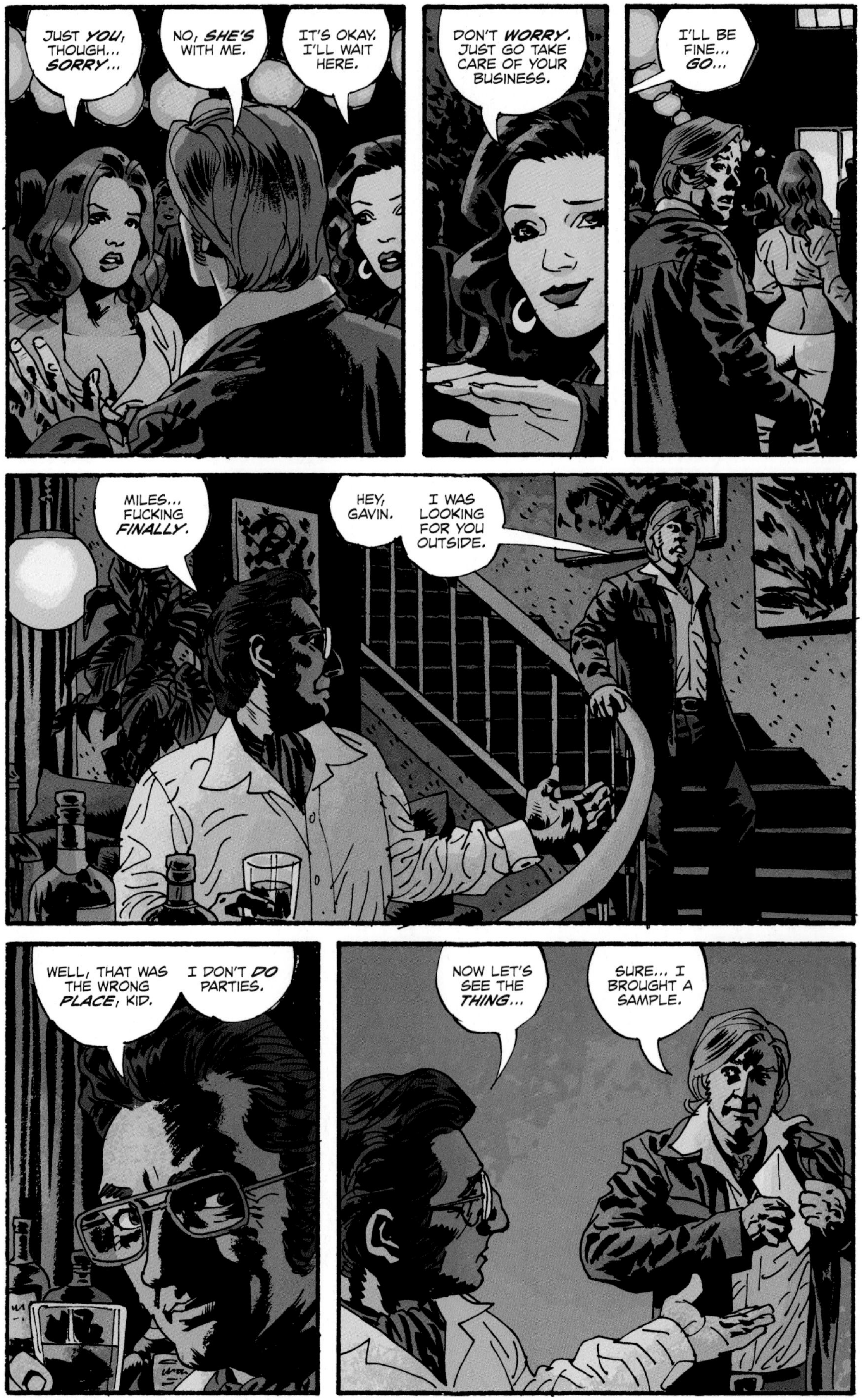
JUST *YOU*, THOUGH... *SORRY*...
NO, *SHE'S* WITH ME.
IT'S OKAY. I'LL WAIT HERE.
DON'T *WORRY*. JUST GO TAKE CARE OF YOUR BUSINESS.
I'LL BE FINE... *GO*...
MILES... FUCKING *FINALLY*.
HEY, GAVIN.
I WAS LOOKING FOR YOU OUTSIDE.
WELL, THAT WAS THE WRONG *PLACE*, KID.
I DON'T *DO* PARTIES.
NOW LET'S SEE THE *THING*...
SURE... I BROUGHT A SAMPLE.

YOU SEE CLAUDIA OUT THERE?

NOT YET, NO...

THAT GIRL... *HUGE* PAIN IN THE ASS...

...BUT STILL WORTH EVERY DIME I PAID YOU.

JESUS... IS THIS...?

IS THIS SOME KINDA *SATANIC* SHIT?

YOUR GUESS IS AS GOOD AS MINE.

WELL, WHAT THE HELL DO YOU WANT FOR IT?

A PART IN YOUR NEXT MOVIE?

AH, KID... KID KID KID...

LET'S NOT PLAY *THAT* GAME AGAIN...

HOW ABOUT WE GO STRAIGHT TO *DOOR NUMBER TWO* ... A SHITLOAD OF CASH?

BECAUSE WE *BOTH* KNOW YOU'RE NOT AN ACTOR...

FINE, THEN... *FIFTY GRAND.*

THAT'S MORE LIKE IT.

SEE, YOU'RE JUST NOT HUNGRY ENOUGH FOR IT ANYMORE, KID.

NOW WHERE THE HELL DID YOU GET THIS?

I *INHERITED* IT... FROM A FRIEND...

HANSEL HAD BEEN BEGGING FORGIVENESS FOR HOURS...

CHANTING THE UNWRITTEN WORDS OVER AND OVER AGAIN...

PLEADING FOR ANOTHER CHANCE...

C'MON... LET'S GET OUTTA HERE...

WHAT *HAPPENED*?

DID YOU DO IT?

FOR THEM TO MAKE THE WORLD TURN HIS WAY...

YEAH, AN' HE'LL *BRAG* TO ONE OF HIS SICK FRIENDS...

WORD'LL GET BACK TO THE *CHURCH*...

DON'T WORRY... THE PLAN'LL *WORK*.

THEY HAD TO HEAR HIM...

SO, WHAT'S *WRONG*, THEN?

MILES...?

THEY HAD TO.

...?

YOU'RE A FRIEND OF *SUZY'S*, RIGHT?

KNOW WHERE I CAN *FIND* HER?

OH... MOTHER*FUCKER.*

MILES... *TALK* TO ME. WHAT *HAPPENED* IN THERE?

YOU... YOU HAVE TO...

YOU HAVE TO *TELL ME* WHAT THE HELL YOU'VE *DONE* TO ME...

OKAY... BUT NOT HERE.

ALL RIGHT... THEY'RE *MOVING*...

DON'T FOLLOW *TOO* CLOSE... WE DON'T WANNA BE *SEEN.*

Chapter Five

LOOKS *CLEAR* 'TIL WE HIT THOSE BUILDINGS.

YOU READY, MAN?

I'D *BETTER* BE...

MILES *SHOULD* HAVE BEEN TERRIFIED.

BUT ALL HE COULD *THINK* WAS...

...AFTER TONIGHT, *SHE* WOULDN'T NEED HIM.

RAT WAS PUMPED... ALMOST *HOPING* THEY'D MEET RESISTANCE IN THE *METHOD COMPOUND*.

BUT MILES WAS DISTRACTED... HALF-LOST IN A FOG...

THE NIGHT BEFORE, JO HAD TOLD HIM THINGS HE HAD TROUBLE BELIEVING...

SO, WHAT... YOU *HYPNOTIZE* PEOPLE...?

THINGS THAT MADE NO SENSE, EVEN TO SOMEONE WHO'D DONE A LOT OF DRUGS.

NO, LOOK, JUST READ *THIS*... YOU'LL SEE.

WHAT *IS* IT? YOUR DIARY?

NO, IT'S AN *ACCOUNTING*... AS BEST AS I CAN DO...

IT TOOK HIM A FEW PAGES TO UNDERSTAND WHAT HE WAS READING...

His hands trembled as he touched me. That's how I knew he'd never give me up, no matter what it cost him.

THE STORIES WERE ALL DIFFERENT, THESE *MEN* WHO'D CROSSED JOSEPHINE'S PATH...

His partner was a member of the Bund, and he'd sent a telegram to an SS commandant in Berlin, describing me in detail.

Hal didn't hesitate to act, and I didn't try to stop him.

...BUT THEIR ENDINGS WERE ALL UNHAPPY. DEATH, INSANITY, PRISON.

It was just a ride to town, but the poor kid was trying to impress me. I never learned his name.

SHE'D LEFT A PATH OF DESTRUCTION IN HER WAKE.

I'VE BEEN TRYING TO REMEMBER THEM ALL...

...BUT THE EARLY YEARS, I DIDN'T *KNOW* ENOUGH.

DIDN'T PAY ATTENTION.

JO... THIS IS CRAZY... YOU'RE NOT *CONTROLLING* ALL THESE --

I *AM*, MILES. EVERYTHING *IN THERE* IS TRUE.

YOU *HAVE* TO BELIEVE ME.

SO, IT'S ALL FAKE...?

YOU FIND WHAT THE LADY *WANTED*?

THINK SO...

WELL *GRAB IT*, THEN, MAN... LET'S *BOOK*.

HANG ON, I DON'T WANNA *TOUCH* IT...

WHAT, IS IT BOUND IN *HUMAN SKIN* OR SOMETHIN'?

SHUT UP.

THOUGHT YOU SAID THEY HAD LIKE *TWENTY* PEOPLE OUT HERE...

THEY DO, USUALLY... BUT BETWEEN GAVIN BRAGGING TO HIS PALS...

...AN' US LEAKING WORD TO OTHER *"COLLECTORS"* THAT SOME SERIOUS SHIT WAS *CHANGING HANDS* TONIGHT...

...LOOKS LIKE OUR *DISTRACTION* WAS BETTER THAN EXPECTED.

I DUNNO... IT'S *WEIRD* THEY WOULDN'T LEAVE A FEW MEN TO GUARD THEIR *CASTLE*...

WAIT... THINK I *SAW*...

OH, JESUS... *SUZY.*

FUCKIN' A...

MILES THOUGHT HE WAS GOING TO SCREAM AND RUN FOR HIS LIFE.

BUT HIS ANGER OVERPOWERED HIS FEAR.

HELP ME CUT HER DOWN.

WHAT?

WE'RE *NOT* LEAVING HER HERE.

THEN HE SAW THE PHOTO OF JO...

...AND REALIZED *WHY* THE WHOLE COMPOUND WAS *DESERTED* TONIGHT...

...AND HIS FEAR TOOK ITS PROPER PLACE.

OH *SHIT.*

SOMETIMES IF HE GOT STONED ENOUGH, JORGE COULD SLEEP AT *HOME*, IN HIS OWN BED.

BUT MOST NIGHTS, HE SAT WATCHING JOSEPHINE'S WINDOWS UNTIL HE PASSED OUT.

PRAYING FOR JUST ONE MORE VISION OF HER... TO HOLD HIM OVER...

BUT HE DIDN'T KNOW HE WAS PRAYING TO THE *WRONG* GODS.

HEY! WHERE YOU FREAKS *GOING?!*

HEY!

JO THOUGHT SHE'D FEEL BETTER AFTER TELLING MILES THE TRUTH... BUT SHE HADN'T.

IF ANYTHING, SHE FELT *MORE* REMOVED FROM THE WORLD...

...AND LESS *HUMAN* THAN SHE HAD IN YEARS.

AND SHE HADN'T TOLD HIM THE WHOLE TRUTH, EVEN.

...?

THAT WAS A GUNSHOT. SHE WAS SURE OF IT.

NOT A CAR BACKFIRING, NOT A FIRECRACKER.

THE STREET IS NOTHING BUT SHADOWS AND SILENCE, BUT SHE CAN FEEL IT.

THE WORLD IS WATCHING HER.

GET BACK IN YOUR ROOM, MONA. I'LL HANDLE THIS.

BUT — BUT — THERE ARE *MEN* IN THE BACKYARD...

MEN IN *ROBES* AND *HOODS*. THEY'RE COMING OVER THE *WALL*.

NONE OF YOU WILL *HURT* THAT WOMAN... DO YOU UNDERSTAND ME?

I AM *RIGHT* BEHIND YOU AND... SHE'S *MINE*.

ABOUT TEN
MINUTES INTO
THE DRIVE...

JESUS!
WATCH
OUT!

...MILES REALIZES
THERE'S SOMETHING
WRONG WITH RAT.

ALMOST
GOT US,
MAN! YOU
FUCKIN' *SEE*
THAT?

EVER SINCE HE
TOUCHED SUZY...

...IT WAS LIKE HE'D
BEEN *DOSED.*

FUCK!
IT STILL
SEES
ME!

AND HE WASN'T JUST
SPEEDING *BACK* TO
JOSEPHINE'S PLACE...

...HE WAS
RUNNING FROM
SOMETHING.

HURRY, MONA.

WHO — WHO *ARE* THESE PEOPLE?

I DON'T KNOW... JUST COME ON...

IS IT THE *MANSON* FAMILY?

NO. OF *COURSE* NOT.

PLEASE, *STOP* TALKING... STOP *THINKING*...

JUST —

NOOO!

UHH —

SHHK

NNHH...
FUCKIN' *STUCK*...

MONA!

YOU
FUCKING --

--BITCH!

AHH -- !

YOU ARE SO
LUCKY...

SO
FUCKING
LUCKY...

IT HAD ALL HAPPENED SO FAST...

BUT *HANSEL* WANTS YOU FOR *HIMSELF.*

...THAT JOSEPHINE DIDN'T EVEN *REALIZE*...

HEY... WHAT...?

...SHE WASN'T *AFRAID* THIS TIME.

WHERE IS SHE?

THEY'RE SEARCHING THE HOUSE... THEY'LL *FIND* HER...

BACK *HERE* – IN THE BAR!

I *HAVE* HER!

HANSEL SMILED *TRULY* FOR THE FIRST TIME IN *DECADES*.

HIS TIME HAD FINALLY COME.

YESSS...

HE FELT THE WORLD ITSELF BEGIN TO *SHATTER* IN ANTICIPATION...

...OR SO HE *THOUGHT*.

SHIT... AHHH...

...RAT, YOU STUPID...

...FUCK...

IT HURTS *INSIDE* WHEN HE MOVES, BUT HE BLOCKS IT OUT... SOMEHOW...

HALF-BLINDED BY HIS OWN BLOOD... STAGGERING TO THE RESCUE...

OOOH... YES YES YES...

IT'S BEEN *FAR* TOO LONG, WOMAN... BUT YOU *STILL* REEK OF THEIR TOUCH...

JUST GET IT *OVER* WITH.

OH NO... WE'LL BE SPENDING *A LOT* OF TIME TOGETHER...

WE HAVE *SO MUCH* TO TALK ABOUT...

LIKE WHERE YOU'VE HIDDEN MY *EYES*...

FOR STARTERS.

SORRY... I WASN'T TALKING TO *YOU.*

WHAT — WHAT IS THAT SMELL?

GASOLINE.

MASTER — FORGIVE ME!

GAAAH — !

NOO!

UUUKK —

AAAAAAHHHHHH!

JO WAS ASHAMED AT HOW MUCH HIS *SCREAMS* PLEASED HER...

AT HOW *EASY* IT WAS TO MAKE A MAN KILL *HIMSELF*...

AT HOW *GOOD* IT FELT BE FREE... UNLEASHED...

MILES HAD BEEN DEAFENED BY RAT'S *MAGNUM* WITH THE FIRST SHOT...

...SO HE DIDN'T HEAR THE GUNFIRE INSIDE THE HOUSE.

NOT THAT HE COULD'VE MOVED ANY FASTER.

THE ONLY THING KEEPING HIM ON HIS FEET AT ALL...

...WAS A DRIVING *NEED* TO SAVE JOSEPHINE.

BUT IF HE'D HEARD THE SHOTS, HE MIGHT'VE SEEN THE MONSTER COMING...

...BEFORE IT WAS TOO LATE.

AHHH -- !

GUU - AHHH - ! NAA -- !

AND THEN IT WAS.

SHE MANAGES TO SAVE A FEW PRECIOUS THINGS...

...BEFORE THE WHOLE HOUSE CATCHES FIRE.

BEFORE HER *VICTORY* TURNS TO *ASH* ALONG WITH IT.

SHE DIDN'T EVEN KNOW HE'D COME BACK.

POOR MILES... POOR FUCKING MILES.

SHE'S ASHAMED AT HOW EASY IT IS TO GET A MAN TO KILL HIMSELF.

OH MILES... YOU BEAUTIFUL FOOL...

YOU DID IT...

YOU SAVED ME.

WHEN THE POLICE AND FIRE TRUCKS ARRIVE, THERE'S NO TRACE OF HER TO BE FOUND.

New Mexico –
Two Months Later

SHE CHARTS THE RIPPLES SHE'S MADE, SHE'S NOT EVEN SURE WHY.

BUT LIKE HANK ALWAYS SAID, NO ONE KNOWS WHY THEY WRITE.

IN THE WAKE OF THE MASSACRE AT HER HOUSE, MILES HAD BECOME A *POSTHUMOUS* CELEBRITY.

THE *ACTOR* CAUGHT IN THE CROSSFIRE OF ANOTHER *HELTER SKELTER*.

THE ONE GOOD MOVIE HE HAD BEEN IN WAS PLAYING TO SELLOUTS AT THE *MIDNIGHT MOVIE* HOUSES.

AND CLAUDIA CONSTANCE WAS GIVING INTERVIEWS ABOUT THEIR "TRAGIC LOVE" ON THE TALK SHOW CIRCUIT.

THE POLICE HAD RAIDED THE METHOD CHURCH'S COMPOUND AND FOUND NOTHING BUT A FEW DAZED AND CONFUSED HIPPY GIRLS.

SHE'D HURT HIM, BUT JO KNEW HANSEL AND HIS INNER CIRCLE WERE STILL OUT THERE.

ESPECIALLY WHEN GAVIN WILDER HAD BEEN FOUND *CHOPPED UP* AND *BURIED* IN THE DESERT.

THEY'D BE COMING FOR HER AGAIN, ONE WAY OR ANOTHER...

HEY, HEY... ALLOW ME, PLEASE...

OR MAYBE... SHE'D BE COMING FOR *THEM.*

THANKS.

HEY, UH... YOU LOOKIN' FOR A RIDE SOMEWHERE?

I MEAN, I SEE THE BAG AN' ALL...

YOU NEED A RIDE? BECAUSE I'M OFFERIN'.

ACTUALLY, HOW ABOUT I JUST TAKE THE KEYS?

Epilogue

In academia, we frown on coincidences... But in real life they happen all the time.

They happen so often you barely even notice, really.

Religious people, people who *believe* in things, they call that fate.

...WHAT THE HELL...?

And the problem with *fate*, these same people will tell you... is it can kill you...

I'd spent weeks driving up and down the highway, checking every Podunk town and *truck stop.*

--SHE MIGHT EVEN BE A *CON ARTIST...*

Talking to every local cop...

BLOND HAIR, KIND OF CURLY...?

SORRY, BUDDY...

...Every used bookstore owner...

...WISH I COULD HELP YA'. NO ONE'S TRIED TO SELL ME NOTHIN' LIKE THAT.

...and way too many bartenders.

ONE MORE?

I was down to my last days on the rental car, down to my last fifty dollars.

And I had described the woman who *robbed me* so many times...

... That I almost thought I was *imagining her* that night.

And it's horrible, I *know*, but my reaction to finding this *dead* woman... Who'd been *placed* in my path somehow...

...Wasn't shock.

It was *relief*.

She hadn't just stolen my money and cards, she'd taken my only *link* to Josephine.

Uncle Dominic's *manuscript*.

I was more desperate to get it back than you can understand.

So when I didn't find it in her bags, I started tearing the car apart.

Which is how the cops found me...

Covered in blood, searching the car of a woman I'd been very publically tracking.

The cop at the station tells me that again and again, like he can't get over it.

...I MEAN, NOT EXACTLY A *CRIMINAL MASTERMIND*, ARE YA?

He tells me how much I'm going to like *jail*, too, and he's right.

They put me in *isolation*, for my own protection.

After *eight months* waiting for trial, I'm not sure if I'm grateful.

But that's where I am when the library cart guy comes by...

HEY, NICKY... CHECK IT OUT...

...And hands me my own worst nightmare.

DIDN'T YOU SAY THIS GUY WAS YOUR UNCLE OR SOMETHIN'?

Trapped in a cell.

A Lost Masterpiece!

THE LOSING SIDE OF ETERNITY

BY DOMINIC RAINES

I start *screaming* ten minutes later.

END OF BOOK TWO

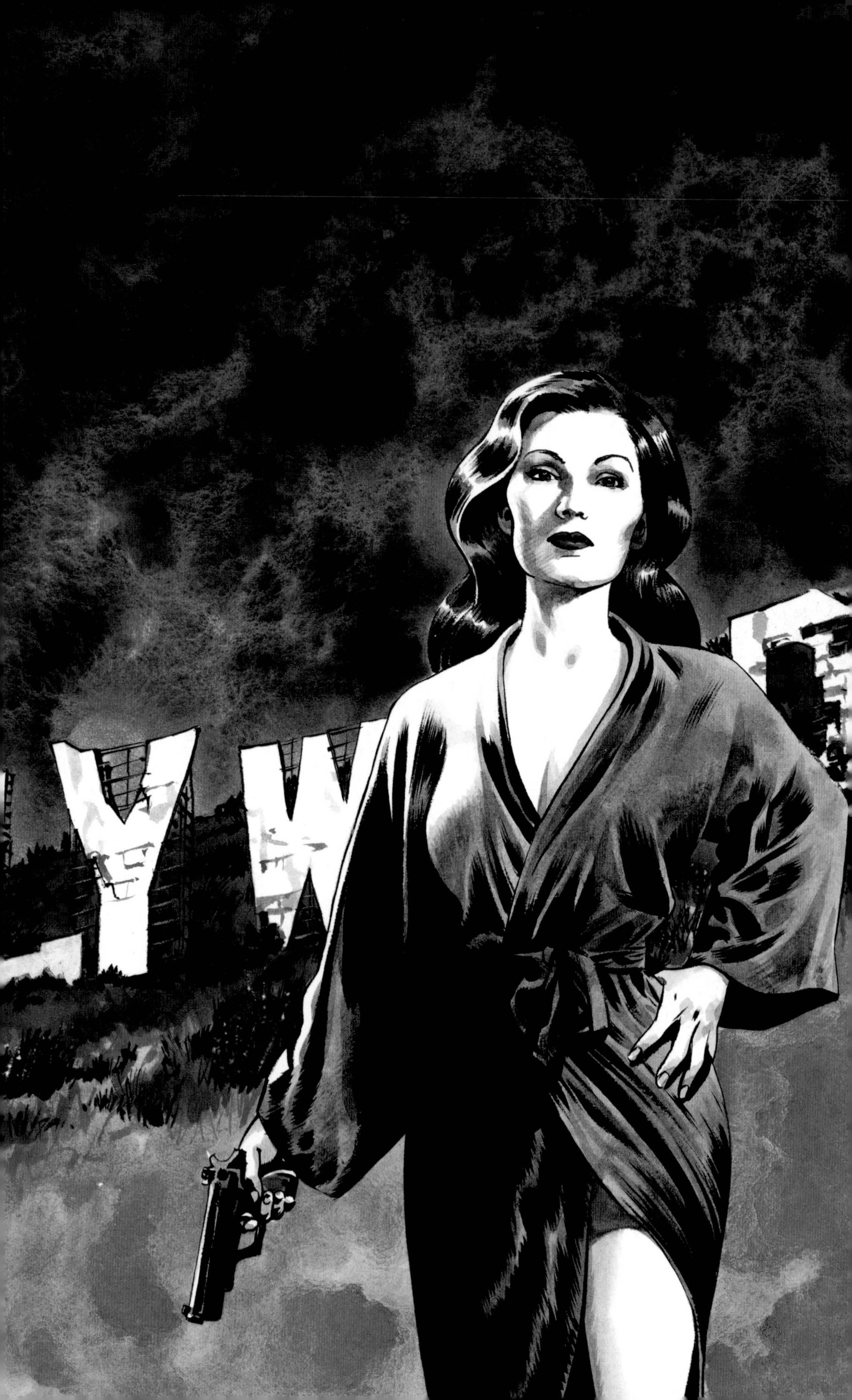

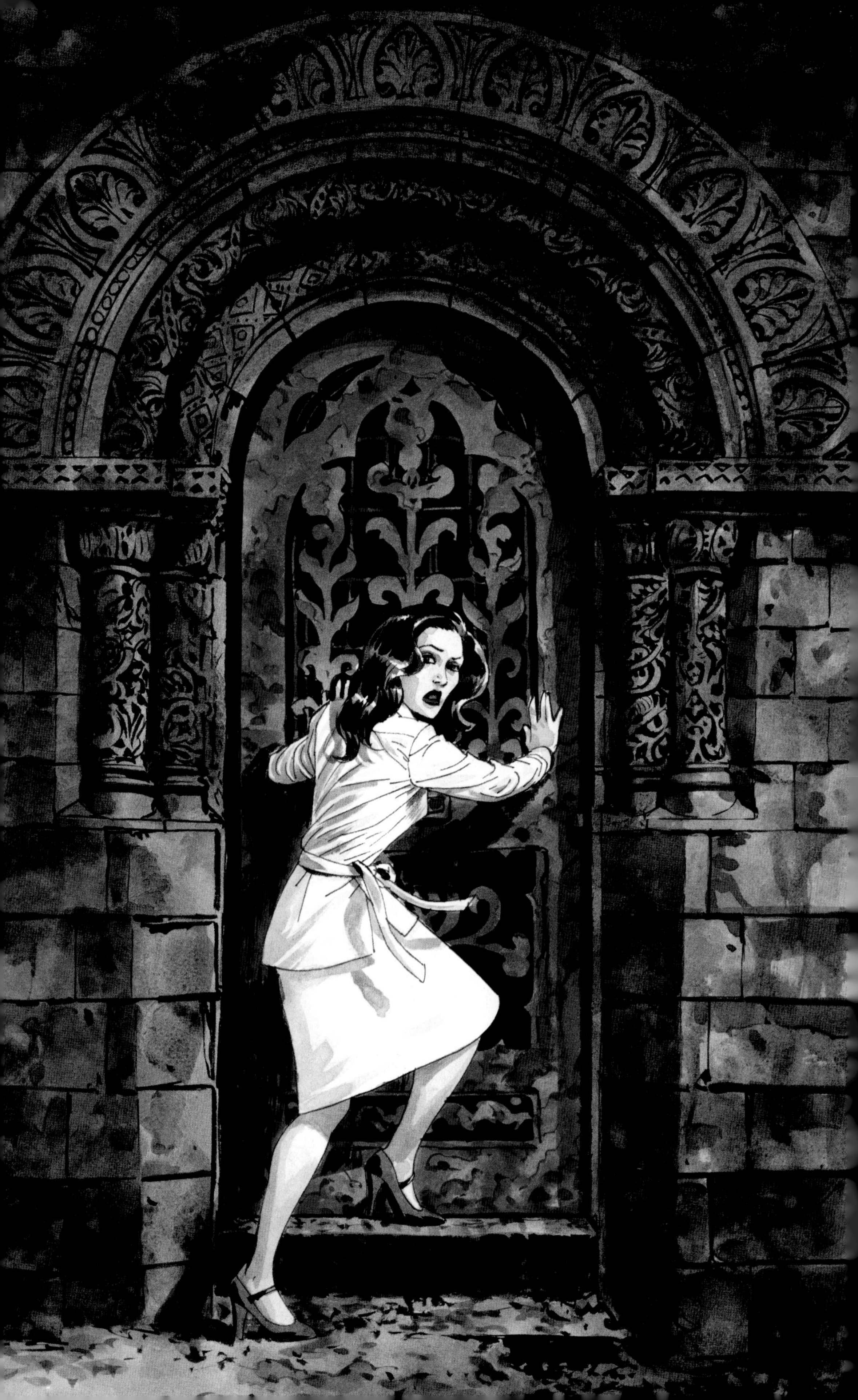

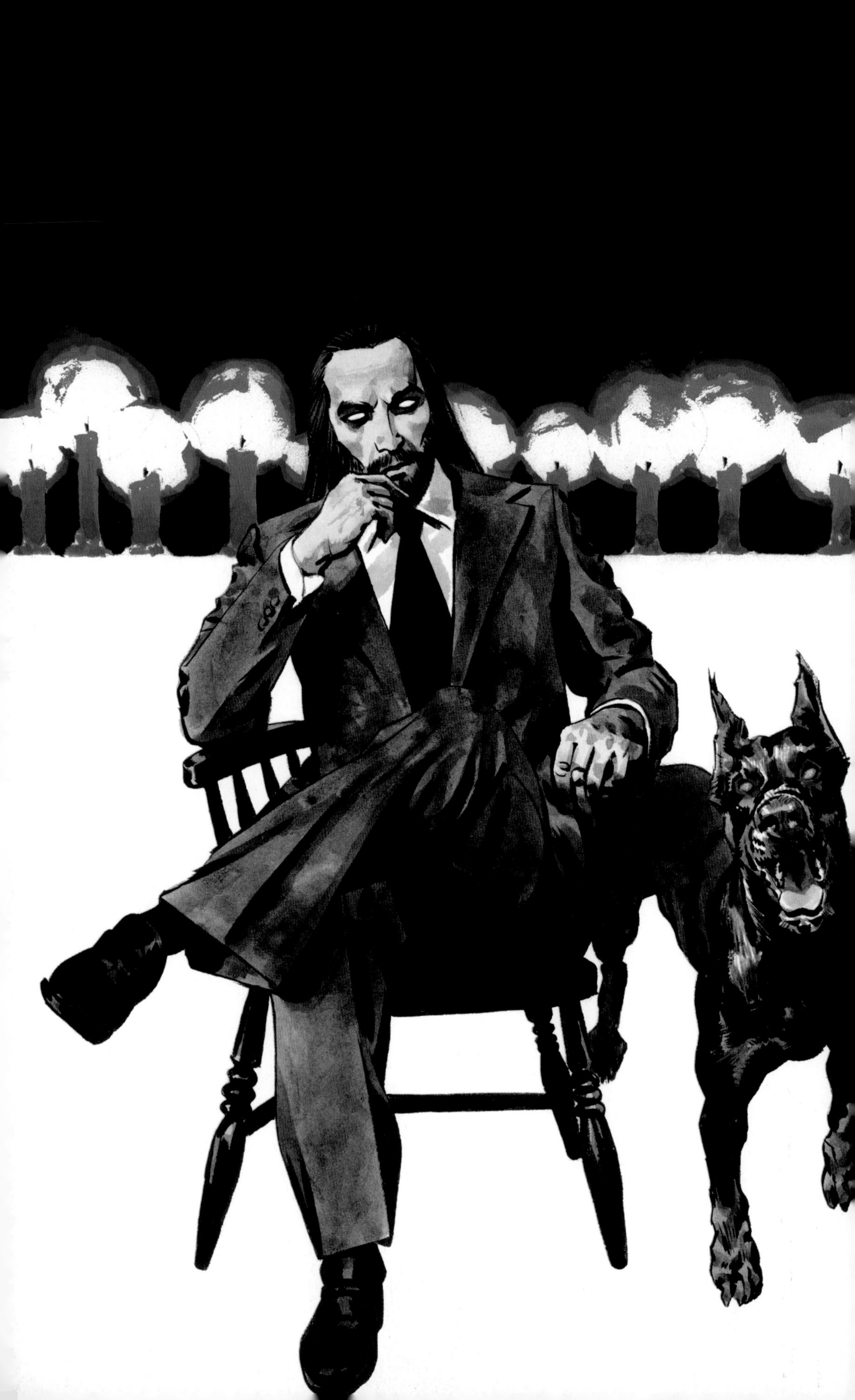

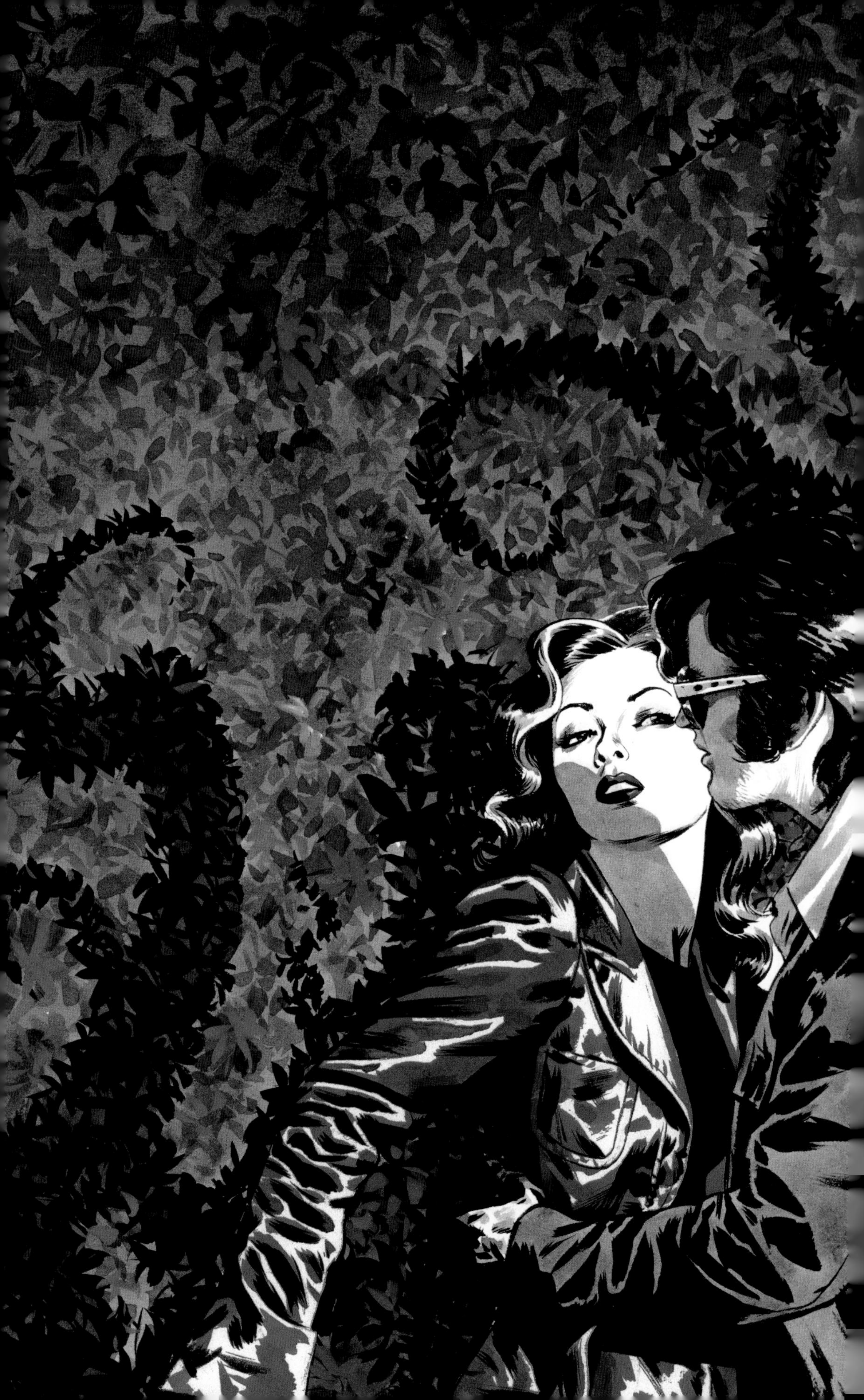

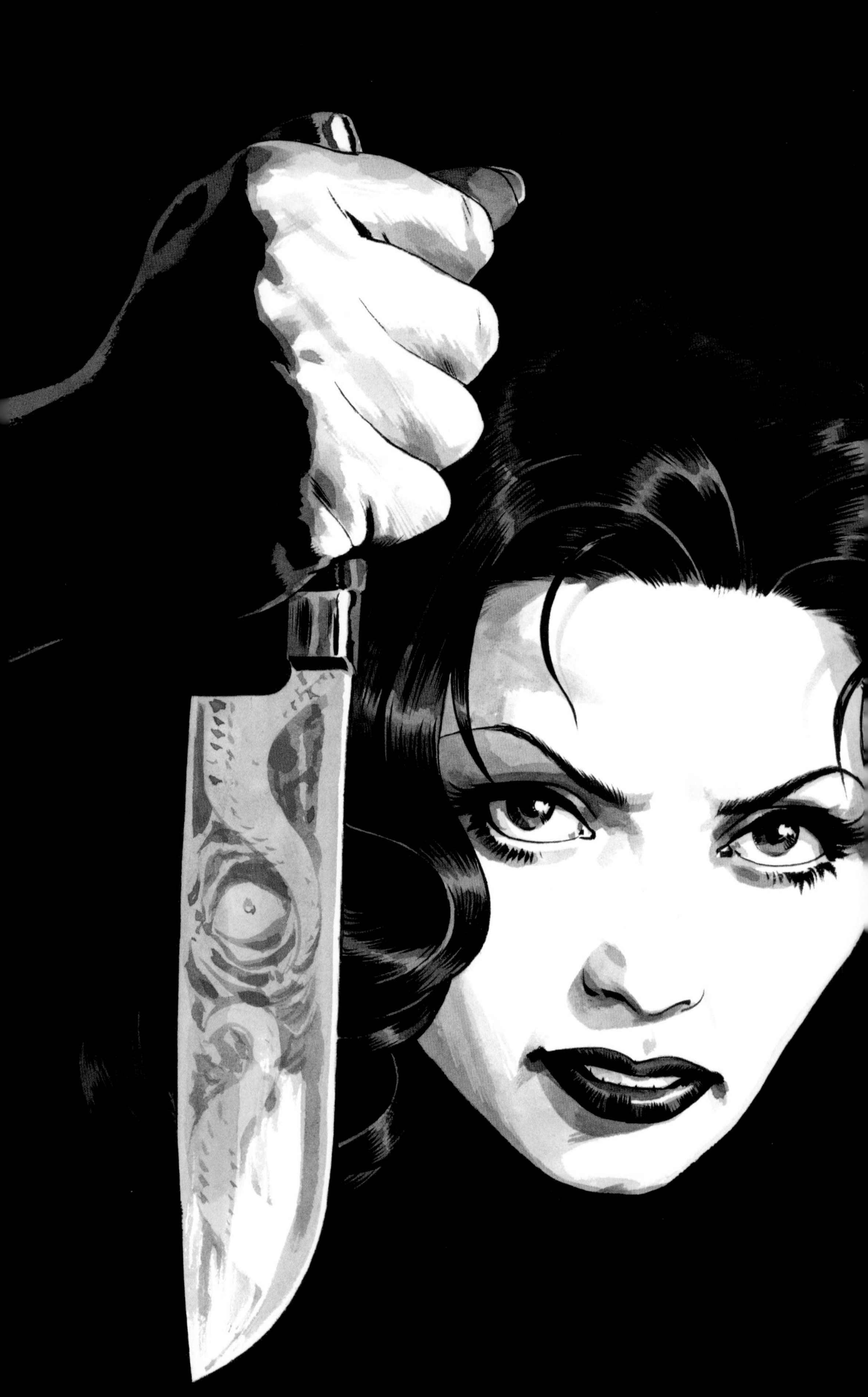

A **CRIMINAL** edition by Ed Brubaker and Sean Phillips

Coward

Introduction by Tom Fontana

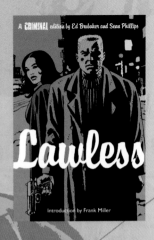

A **CRIMINAL** edition by Ed Brubaker and Sean Phillips

Lawless

Introduction by Frank Miller

A **CRIMINAL** edition by Ed Brubaker and Sean Phillips

The Dead and the Dying

Introduction by John Singleton

A **CRIMINAL** edition by Ed Brubaker and Sean Phillips

Bad Night

Introduction by Ken Bruen

CRIMINAL
The Deluxe Edition

Ed Brubaker Sean Phillips
Introduction by Dave Gibbons

A **CRIMINAL** edition by Ed Brubaker and Sean Phillips

The Sinners

Introduction by Ian Rankin

A **CRIMINAL** edition by Ed Brubaker and Sean Phillips

The Last Of The Innocent

Introduction by Patton Oswalt

ED BRUBAKER
SEAN PHILLIPS
INCOGNITO

INTRODUCTION BY
BILL HADER

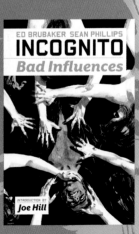

ED BRUBAKER SEAN PHILLIPS
INCOGNITO
Bad Influences

INTRODUCTION BY
Joe Hill

Also available

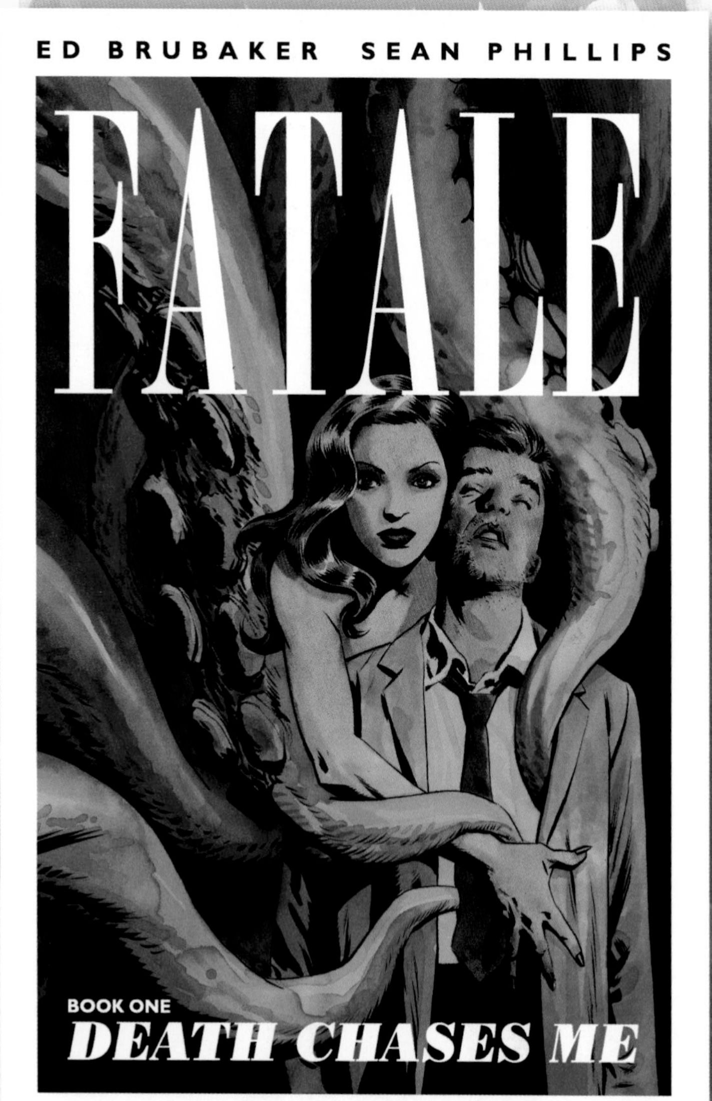
ED BRUBAKER SEAN PHILLIPS
FATALE
BOOK ONE
DEATH CHASES ME

FATALE Book One